Small Town
Secrets

by

Riley Scott

Bella
BOOKS

2014

Bella Books, Inc.
P.O. Box 10543
Tallahassee, FL 32302

Printed in the United States of America on acid-free paper.

First Bella Books Edition 2014

Editor: Katherine V. Forrest
Cover Designer: Judith Fellows

ISBN: 978-1-59493-424-7

Other Bella Books by Riley Scott

Conservative Affairs

Acknowledgments

A story such as this one could not come without having seen, firsthand, the prejudices held by many in Small Town, America. Unfortunately, this prejudice and discrimination still exists, and stories such as this are told to shed light into this darkness, educate, and most importantly share a message of acceptance and love with young girls who may be struggling in similar environments. In writing this book, I was reminded of the work of generations of social justice pioneers whose fight for equality has paved the way for changing minds and hearts across our society. As we see movement toward societal acceptance, it is encouraging. In light of this, I thank all who have used their voices and resources to further the conversation and speak out against discrimination. In my home state, I extend my gratitude to Equality New Mexico for the great work they continue to do. Additionally, I recognize that this story could not have come into existence without the loved ones in my own life who have exceeded my expectations of mere acceptance and met me instead with unconditional love and full support.

About the Author

In addition to having published poetry and short stories, Riley Scott has worked as a grant and press writer and holds a degree in journalism. A chunk of life spent in the Bible Belt has given her a close-up look at the struggle for balance between love and church, home and state. She is a proud New Mexican with a strong love for green chile, dogs and lively literature.

Dedication

For every girl who has ever questioned her identity, for all who have faced discrimination and judgment, for all who are still struggling with acceptance, and for those who have overcome. Most importantly, for the wonderful individuals who have peppered my journey toward acceptance, love, and inclusion with humor, support, and encouragement, and without whose inspiration I could not tell a story so close to my own journey.

CHAPTER ONE

Blazing past a sea of green jerseys, one stood out in stark white and blue. Zoe Michelson, the new starting guard for the Bulldogs, drove through the lane and easily finished a textbook layup.

"Michelson is on fire tonight!" one announcer's voice boomed excitedly. "With only five games left in the season, it's go time. And these girls came out to play!"

"I sure am glad to see that," the other announcer agreed. "I was a little worried when they lost Weston that they just wouldn't bounce back. But tonight they're playing with renewed fire and you almost wouldn't even notice Weston isn't out on the court."

The words stung, but they echoed exactly what Jordan Weston already knew—she had been replaced.

She picked up the remote and clicked off the television set. There was only so much she could take on a night like tonight.

Sure, she was happy for Zoe—who had been her best friend for two years—and for the rest of the team. It did not change the fact that she was jealous and bitter.

She glanced down at her left knee and wanted to scream.

"If only you could have held on for two more years," she whispered sadly. "Just two years and I wouldn't have asked you for more."

But, injuries came whether or not you were ready for them, and this one had come with the promise of never playing basketball again.

Leaning back against the couch, she tried to block the negativity out of her mind. She replayed all of the pep talks she had received.

"There's more to life than basketball."

"It'll give you time to focus on your studies—or maybe find a nice boy and settle down."

"Keep your head up. You still have big things ahead of you."

"I don't know why you're so upset. It's just a game. There are a million other things you can do."

"You're still a part of the team."

The words had come pouring in from family members and friends, but they had fallen flat against the harshness of reality. Then, the words of encouragement came less frequently, and despite all their promises of support, in the past several months people had disappeared one by one.

Some commented on how she had changed. Others said they missed her smile and upbeat attitude. The truth was that she was trying to adjust, but it was difficult. And it was even more difficult when she had to face it all alone.

Of course she had changed. The life she had spent years building had suddenly disappeared. From the time she first picked up a basketball at the age of five, she had known what it was to dream, to set goals, and to fight for what she wanted. Summer after summer, she had gone to basketball camps and played on traveling teams.

Each year there were new faces, new teammates, and always new skills to learn. But one thing remained, and that was her passion. She had spent countless hours in the gym to make sure she got a scholarship to play on the collegiate level, and when it finally happened, all of her hard work had come to fruition.

Her teammates in college had been her best friends, but even they had drifted away when she was no longer one of them. Eventually, she had given up traveling with the team. It hurt a little too much to sit on the end of the bench with no hope of ever getting into the game. The minute she stepped away, they stopped caring.

Her phone buzzed, bringing her momentarily out of her pity party.

She unlocked the screen and read the text from her mom. *Watching the game and thought of you. Have you checked out that singles group?*

The words brought a slight smile to her face. Her mother kept trying to push her into what she called a singles group. The message was twofold and exceedingly clear—go to church and meet someone new.

"Your clock should be ticking," her mother had urged last weekend, once again suggesting that it was time to put away the foolishness of her childhood and start thinking about marriage and babies. After all, as far as her parents were concerned, no one in this town made it to their mid-twenties without marrying unless something was wrong with them.

While she had no interest in either joining a church or in dating someone at the moment, she relented. She had already checked it out, giving in to the fact that her mother would not stop pressing.

I looked up the time and place, she texted her mother. *I got all of the information. I'll check it out.*

If it was the only way to get her mother off her back, she would give it a shot. She could go, tell her mother that it was awful, and never have to hear about it again.

* * *

Jordan sat in the parking lot of the coffee shop where the SLIC group was supposed to meet. She was early—as always, and she was more nervous than she felt was appropriate.

Again she turned over the pamphlet in her hands. "Singles Living in Christ," it read. Fake-looking smiles shone up at her from the faces of young males and females on the pages. It all seemed too forced, and she felt out of place. She had no idea what she was doing here, and she contemplated simply driving off and going home.

Stubbornly, she gripped the wheel. She would do this, because she had said she would. Never in her life had she been one to give her word and not follow through with the commitment. Even if it was the worst thing ever, she would give it an hour of her life. Besides, it wasn't as if she had anything better to do with her time. It was this or Netflix, and somehow this seemed a little less sad than a young twenty-something sitting all alone in a dark apartment, eating popcorn and watching TV on the Internet.

As new cars started to pull into the parking lot, she watched. She was parked far enough away that they wouldn't easily see her, and she had the opportunity to scope out the group before entering.

A nerdy-looking guy in his thirties got out of one of the cars, looking far too excited to be joining a bunch of other single losers for coffee. Jordan shook her head, attempting to clear the thoughts. Tonight she was one of the losers, and she was going to have to think with more optimism.

Each person who stepped out of their car looked less and less promising to Jordan. Not that she wanted to date anyone here, but she did want to at least have the possibility of meeting some people she might want to hang out with later. There seemed to be no chance of that.

She stole a glance at the clock. The group was starting in three minutes. Taking a deep breath, she got out of the car.

It was a simple little building, but they did have decent drinks. If nothing else, she figured she would do a little people watching and sip a nice cup of chai.

Still, calming her nerves proved to be more difficult a feat than she had anticipated. She looked down at her shaking hands and chided herself for being nervous. There was no reason for it. These people were geeks anyway.

"Don't tell me you're deciding whether or not to run away?" a woman's voice asked, startling her.

Jordan turned around quickly and found herself eye-to-eye with a beautiful girl with long sandy brown hair that flowed freely and whose blue eyes sparkled with a hint of mischief. From her genuine, welcoming smile to her ripped jeans and ball cap, she seemed as out of place here as Jordan felt. She took a small step back. At her height, she wasn't quite used to someone standing as tall as she did.

Suddenly remembering that the girl had asked her a question, she tried to answer. "I guess I was," she said with a shrug. "It's my first time here."

"I know it is," the girl replied. "I would have recognized you otherwise. Anyway, I'm Taylor." She held out her hand.

"It's nice to meet you. I'm Jordan."

Jordan couldn't put her finger on any specific reason, but she liked Taylor already. There was a welcoming warmth about her, and yet she still seemed like the type of person Jordan could hang out with and have fun.

The two fell in step together as they approached the building.

"It's not so bad, I promise," Taylor said, leaning in to whisper the words.

A slight shiver went through Jordan's body as Taylor's words seemed to slide over her skin. It was as if there was a magnetism that drew her to Taylor, and she immediately felt at ease in her presence.

She took a deep breath as they walked through the doors. To her surprise, she realized that her nerves had calmed, and she was actually excited to be here.

As the room filled with people, Taylor gave Jordan a smile. "Well, I've got to kick this thing off tonight. Callie, who usually leads it, is out of town. I'll catch up with you after to see how you liked it, though."

Jordan nodded, hoping her words were a promise—not merely spoken to appease her nerves.

Taylor walked confidently to the front of the room. "Good evening, everyone," she said with a smile that Jordan was sure could have landed her a job as a model.

"For those of you who don't know, I'm Taylor Reeves, and I'll be leading the discussion tonight. If you have any questions, feel free to ask. This is not a lecture; it's a discussion."

Her voice was clear and cool, Jordan noted, and it lacked the accent of so many from Kansas. She wanted to know where Taylor was originally from—and what she was doing in a place like this.

Before she could get too deep into the list of things she wanted to know about this mysterious Bible study leader, a teenage boy in the back of the room raised his hand.

Jordan followed Taylor's gaze. He looked far too young to be in the group, but no one seemed to think he was out of place. Maybe this place was accepting and open after all, Jordan thought.

"Reeves?" he asked. "Like, are you related to Pastor Reeves?"

Taylor gave a slight laugh as she nodded. "I am. He's my father."

Jordan's eyebrows shot up at the revelation. Her father was the man running the show at the largest church in town, and it was quite the feat in the Bible Belt for any church to beat out the rest. Stifling a giggle, she thought of all the gossip she'd heard about preacher's kids—and all the case studies that had proven the stereotype of how wild they could be to be true. It was enough to spark in her an even greater interest in Taylor. There was something entirely fascinating about the girl. From the way she moved with such confidence, quietly and beautifully commanding the attention of everyone in the room.

Throughout the course of the study group, Jordan couldn't take her eyes off Taylor. She took notes, hanging on every word.

As Taylor spoke about what it meant to truly be a friend to someone, to build them up with words of encouragement, Jordan clung to every point she made. Though they were lessons she had heard taught in every youth group she had ever attended, it felt as though she was uncovering some new truth she had never heard.

Although she could not pinpoint the reason, she felt that this girl was out of place here. Sure, she gracefully and confidently maneuvered her way through the lesson, and it was obvious that everyone here adored her. Yet, there was something about her that was so unlike most of the people that Jordan had grown to dislike in Kansas.

It seemed as if everyone in the area was so arrogant and self-righteous. Taylor was a preacher's daughter, but she showed no signs of such egotistical and judgmental behavior.

There had to be more to her story, and Jordan wanted to find out all about it. Unfortunately, the Bible study drew to a close, and even though Jordan wanted to stick around, she felt like it might be awkward.

Even so she waited in the back of the room for a few minutes. Taylor was surrounded by a group of people who all seemed to have questions. She heard invitations for coffee and lunch dates, and once again she felt all too alone. Not wanting to appear to be a stalker or a strange loner, she turned to leave.

She almost bumped into a scrawny and pale, bearded man who she was pretty sure never emerged from his house except to buy a video game or to come to these meetings. From his crumpled polo shirt to his baggy jeans, she judged every aspect of his appearance in an instant. Immediately, she scolded herself for her quick judgment and tried to bypass him.

"Hi," he said, with a smile that made Jordan suddenly wish he'd stopped with the awkward stare. "I'd been hoping to come over and meet you."

She managed a sweet smile. "Hi, I'm Jordan," she said. "It's nice to meet you."

"I'm Jacob," he said, his smile growing. "We both have J names. Isn't that cool?"

She nodded, not knowing what else to do, reminding herself not to be quite so rude or quick to jump to conclusions. But at this point he was not the one she wanted to be talking to. If she were honest, there was only one person in the room she even thought she could befriend.

Still, she stood and listened as he rattled off the fact that he worked in IT and loved to spend his weekends doing Civil War reenactments.

No surprises there.

Nonetheless, she made polite responses, but as soon as she saw an opportunity, she wrapped up the chat. This was exactly what she had hoped to avoid at this group meeting. Apparently, there were people who treated the Bible study as a speed dating group.

"I've got to go," she said, before adding, "I really enjoyed meeting you."

As she exited the building, she hoped she didn't look like exactly what she was—a girl running for cover.

"Jordan!"

Even though she had only heard the voice for the first time tonight, she recognized it immediately. Turning around with a smile, she saw Taylor following her out the door.

"We didn't scare you away already, did we?" Taylor asked.

Jordan laughed. "No, not at all. I just came out here to get some air and head home."

"I see," Taylor said. "Well, are you headed home immediately?"

Jordan recognized the hint of an invitation in the question, and weighed her options. She could sit on the couch in sweatpants, covered in Cheez-It crumbs and watching Netflix. Or she could go out and try to make a new friend.

Taylor filled the silence as Jordan thought about her response. "I'm not trying to be pushy," she said. "I just wanted a chance to get to know you a little better."

"Standard preacher's daughter responsibilities?" Jordan asked playfully, hoping that legitimately was not the case.

Taylor laughed in response. "Not quite," she said. "I don't really do the whole preacher's daughter responsibility thing on a regular basis. Tonight was a one-time deal. There's just something about you that makes me think we could be friends."

"Well, then I guess I'm in," Jordan said. "What did you have in mind?"

Taylor gestured to a red Ford truck sitting on the edge of the lot. "Hop in, and I'll show you," she said.

"Is this where you take me out to a field and chop me into tiny pieces?" Jordan asked.

"We're not really *that* kind of church," Taylor said, laughing. "That's the church across the street. You're safe with us."

Jordan laughed along with Taylor, not sure how to take her humor.

"Stop being so suspicious and come on."

Jordan shrugged. "All right, you talked me into it," she said.

The truth was, Taylor could have talked her into pretty much anything at that point, she was almost certain.

They got into the truck, and Taylor put it into first gear.

Jordan watched her carefully, taking note of every little detail. She was a walking mystery, and Jordan wanted to know so much more. Her Chiefs ball cap and her mannerisms as she shifted gears seemed somewhat masculine, but her perfectly applied—albeit subtle—makeup left no question about the fact that she was definitely quite feminine.

"So where are you from?" she asked, breaking into Jordan's thought process.

"I'm from here," Jordan said, as if admitting so automatically made her a loser.

"Don't be so quick to knock it," Taylor said. "At least you have a home."

Jordan's curiosity was piqued. "What do you mean by that?"

"I'm a bit of a tumbleweed," Taylor admitted. "We've moved around so much that I'm not really sure I have a place I call home. I guess if I had to pick, Oklahoma felt more like home than anywhere, but even that was temporary. I'm not much of a settler."

Jordan let the thought marinate for a while, before coming to the conclusion that moving around sounded like an adventure. Immediately she wanted to know more and as she tried to sift through her questions and determine which ones were most important, she cocked her head to the side.

"I'd love to know the thoughts behind that look," Taylor said with an amused smile.

"Sorry," Jordan said, blushing and snapping her focus back into the moment. "I was just curious about what it was like living so many different places. I mean, I've only ever lived around here."

She hoped her voice didn't give away just how enamored she was with this girl. The last thing she wanted to do was appear to be that little kid following around the cool crowd.

Taylor's soft smile put her nerves at ease. "We'll chat all about it inside," she said, motioning to the diner across the parking lot. "Does this look okay to you?"

"That works for me," Jordan said with a shrug. She didn't really care. To be honest, she was just happy to have a friend— even if just for a while.

Inside, they sat at a booth in the back. With the soft glow of parking lot lights in the background, Jordan felt more at home than she had in weeks.

"Would you have any interest in splitting some chili cheese fries?" Taylor asked with a hint of a mischievous grin.

The look made Jordan laugh. It was as if they were breaking the rules.

Jordan looked down self-consciously, considering the offer. "I really shouldn't," she said.

"Why on earth not?" Taylor asked.

"I'm going to have to start watching what I eat a lot more," Jordan admitted somewhat shyly. "I'm not getting near as much exercise as my body is used to."

"You look like you're in good shape to me. I'd love to have that body, actually."

Jordan blushed at the compliment. For reasons she couldn't explain, Taylor's admiration of her body made her heart soar. She took the moment to look Taylor up and down in curiosity.

"You have a pretty nice body, too," she commented, looking at those long legs and the way her trim hourglass figure was displayed in something as simple as jeans and a fitted T-shirt.

"Thanks," Taylor said casually, accepting the compliment with ease. "Then there's no reason for us to skip out on the fries."

Her logic was simple, but Jordan figured a little indulgence wouldn't hurt.

"Okay, I'll eat some of them," she conceded.

As their fries came out, Jordan got lost in conversation. All of her previous inhibitions slipped away as the two of them chatted into the evening about movies, TV, the various towns Taylor had lived in—and all sorts of sports other than basketball, to Jordan's relief.

Jordan glanced at her watch. "I better head home," she said reluctantly. "I have a big paper to write for tomorrow's class."

A slow smile spread across Taylor's face.

"What is it?" Jordan asked.

"Nothing really," Taylor said with a shrug. "You just reminded me how old I am."

Jordan furrowed her brow. Surprisingly, they hadn't broached the subject of age in all that they had covered. "How old are you?" she asked innocently.

"Way to put a girl on the spot," Taylor teased. "Twenty-nine."

"That's not old at all," Jordan retorted.

"Sometimes it feels like it," Taylor replied. "But either way, let me get you back to your car."

Taylor dropped some money on the table, and Jordan started to protest.

"My treat," Taylor said both cheerfully and firmly.

Jordan thanked her and side by side they walked out of the diner.

Once they were back in the coffee shop parking lot, Jordan was hesitant to get out of the truck. It seemed as though she had finally found a friend, and as lonely as she had been, she didn't want to give up that feeling just yet.

"What's your number?" Taylor asked.

Jordan smiled. Taylor wanted to be her friend, too, or at least it seemed that way. Quickly, she rattled off her number and watched Taylor enter it into her phone. Taylor gave Jordan her number as well, and Jordan leaned over and hugged Taylor.

She had never been overly affectionate, but it just felt right in the moment. To her relief, Taylor did not seem to think the gesture odd. Instead, she returned the hug and warmly said, "I had a wonderful time tonight. Let's hang out again soon."

"Definitely," Jordan agreed, getting out of the vehicle.

On her drive home, she felt a twinge of hope. Perhaps all was not lost since her recent removal from the basketball team. For the first time in months, she felt as though the future had possibility. Maybe she had a whole new life waiting up ahead of her.

CHAPTER TWO

The silver moonlight lighting her small backyard provided the perfect serene backdrop for the way Taylor was feeling. She had hated this town ever since she moved here. The people were as fake as they were set into their cliques.

Sure, they were all warm on the outside, with their superficial smiles and quick hugs. Yet, they were the most judgmental people she had ever encountered, and that was saying a lot considering she had church-hopped since she was a baby.

She had gone into tonight's meeting with her usual pep talk. She would go into the room, she would show genuine feeling and she would go home. It had been her theory that all these people really needed was someone genuine, and slowly it seemed to have been making people take notice. Not that she wanted attention; she just wanted to show them what it was like to be a real person—one who didn't care what everyone else in the room thought or how things appeared to outside eyes.

Now, she wondered if she was being hypocritical as she let another sip of rum slide down the back of her throat. She swallowed the bitter liquid and stared at her backyard.

The feeling of camaraderie in this place was foreign to her, but it gave her hope. There was something special about Jordan Weston. She had no doubt about that.

Jordan was the first person that Taylor had actually carried on a legitimate conversation with in the four months since she had been in Kansas, aside from family. It was the first time she felt as though there was someone in the godforsaken town that she might be able to trust someday.

The feeling made her smile as she took another sip. She thought about Jordan's beautiful smile, and the way that her adorable dimple showed when she laughed. The girl was breathtaking. But, more than that, she was real.

She glanced down at her phone, and briefly contemplated sending Jordan a text message. She had meant every word when she said she wanted to hang out with Jordan again. But, she resisted the urge. There was no need to scare that girl off right now.

Besides, Jordan could not provide her the solace from her loneliness that she longed for. Sure, Jordan could provide friendship, but one look in the girl's eyes had told Taylor that anything else was off limits. It was clear that Jordan was far too innocent to even consider anything different.

She let out a slow sigh and lit a cigarette. Taking a drag, she felt the nicotine swim through her body, relaxing her nerves. Thankful once again that, although the house was tiny, she was able to afford a place of her own, a sanctuary, thanks to the church providing it for nearly nothing in monthly rent.

In the alley, she saw a car drive slowly by her house. She watched as the head in the driver's seat turned and stared at her. Quickly, she moved the cigarette out of plain view and waited for the driver to move on down the street.

For the millionth time since she moved here, she simply wanted to scream. This town was full of small-town, small-minded busybodies who were more concerned with what she was doing than with their own lives. She guessed it was always that way in a small town, but as a pastor's daughter, it felt like the scrutiny would never end.

There was always someone else to please and someone's approval to win. She missed Oklahoma and her friends back home. She thought of her childhood best friend Amy, who had been one of the few to simply accept her. With Amy, she had never needed to win approval. She had never needed to explain herself. They had just bonded easily and effortlessly, and had stayed close throughout the years—through every stage of life, through every heartache.

It wasn't that easy here. People didn't seem to accept. They judged, just as so many people had done all her life. They had a preconceived notion of what made a "good preacher," and that always included picture-perfect children.

In her mind, she replayed all the little lessons her mother had tried to teach her brothers and her through repetition as children.

"Sit up straight."

"Wear that dress. It makes you look pretty, and we all know we need to look pretty."

"You can't let anyone see you cry. It looks bad on your father if he has unhappy children."

It was always a show, and it probably always would be. But, right here, right now, she was hers alone. There was no one she had to answer to, and there was no one to tell her what was proper.

Proper. She hated the word. It seemed as even speaking it was too stuffy, too disingenuous. She and her brothers had learned long ago how to put on a proper face, while hiding everything else. It had been their tactic of survival and possibly the only way they had stayed sane. Although they occasionally fought, they had been each other's allies in hiding details from their parents. As she put out her cigarette, she felt like that same little kid again, hiding out and hoping mommy and daddy didn't find out.

Once again, she let her mind drift back to the night she had enjoyed. The piercing green of Jordan's eyes as she smiled would surely haunt her dreams for nights to come, but she pushed that thought aside and focused instead on how easily their conversation had flowed.

By the end of the night, she felt as if she had known Jordan for years—not hours.

That was the type of friendship she had been missing—craving, even.

She heard her phone buzz, breaking her out of her dreamlike thoughts.

Her smile grew as she looked at the screen.

I know it's probably a little weird to text you so soon, the text from Jordan read. *I just wanted to say thank you again. It meant a lot to me to find a friend tonight.*

There was something so raw and honest in the text message. Although it was a simple grouping of words, Taylor could read into it the underlying loneliness. It seemed that Jordan was searching for companionship just as much as Taylor was. The thought broke her heart, as she couldn't imagine a girl that sweet being so alone. However, it also brought about hope that maybe each could be the friend that both were looking for.

Leaning back in her chair, she took another sip from the bottle, carefully thinking through her reply.

* * *

She knew it was late, but her curiosity was getting the best of her. Damn her curiosity.

Trying to stifle her need to know if Taylor Reeves had screwed up her group was like trying to convince a heroin addict that she didn't need another hit. Unable to suppress her need any longer, Callie Wilkins quickly grabbed her cell phone.

After one ring, an obviously sleepy Chris picked up his phone.

"Callie, how are you?" he asked through a yawn.

"I'm good," she replied quickly, wanting to get to the point of the call. "I'm ready to be home, though. How was the group meeting tonight?"

"You make it sound like a cult," he said with a lazy laugh.

She found no humor in his comment. "I do not. But, seriously, how was it?" With each minute she had to wait to get the news that Taylor had screwed up, yet again, she was growing more impatient.

"It was pretty good," he said. "There was a hot new girl there."

"Are you really there for the girls?" she asked with irritation. "Never mind," she cut him off before he could answer. "I don't have time to get into that."

She took a deep breath, reminding herself to calm down. She didn't want him to call her a gossip again. He did that far too often.

"What do you mean it was pretty good?" she asked, knowing he'd crack under pressure.

"What do you really want to know?" he asked, clearly tired and not wanting to go through her usual twenty questions.

That was the beauty of a good friend, she thought. They knew your weaknesses, and she knew one of hers was having to know as much information as possible on her enemies. She didn't know that she would exactly classify Taylor as an enemy, but she definitely didn't like the girl with all her big-city ways and the way she seemed to think she could waltz in here and steal Callie's territory.

She sighed. "I want to know how Taylor did," she admitted. She should be ashamed at how transparent she was, but she didn't really care at the moment.

Chris let out a small laugh. "She did fine," he said. "Why don't you like her?"

"I never said I don't like her," Callie quipped.

She could just picture Chris's brow furrowing quizzically. "You don't have to say it, Cal. We can all see it. Even she sees it."

"Well, she isn't the friendliest person I've ever met. It's not like she tries all that hard." Even Callie could hear the way her voice escalated to an unnatural pitch. She worked to bring it back down. "Sorry," she muttered.

Chris was full-out laughing now. "I think she's pretty friendly. She's always been nice to me, but in the spirit of friendship, I'll indulge you in a little bit of information."

Callie felt the corners of her lips creep up into a slight smile. Although she'd never admit it to anyone willingly, juicy gossip was her favorite pastime, and she hoped this would be good.

"Go ahead," she urged.

"Well, when she left, she went to hang out with the new girl I was telling you about," he said. "That's about all that was out of the norm."

"She's usually kind of a loner," Callie said, contemplating. "I wonder if the new girl is a friend of hers."

"I don't know," Chris said. "But I think Taylor's only a loner because you all push her away."

Callie felt her blood boil. Chris was supposed to be her friend and take her side. She knew she was being irrational, but she didn't care.

"Good night," she said.

As she slammed her cell phone down on the counter, she wanted to scream. She didn't understand why everyone was so enamored with Taylor Reeves. Sure she was pretty and she was the exciting new girl from a far-off place. Callie's thoughts were filled with bitterness.

She had spent years working to build the young adults' group. This was her home. This was her church, and she didn't like someone stomping all over her territory. Even more than that, she sensed Taylor had a secret she was hiding. Callie was determined to find out what it was.

In her head, she heard her best friend's amused voice. *"If there's a secret within a hundred yards, this one will sniff it out."*

It was the truth, and it was a truth of which she was damn proud.

CHAPTER THREE

The loud crash of a slamming door jolted Jordan awake. It was completely dark outside, and for a moment she was lost in confusion.

She rolled over from her spot on the couch to see her roommate bounding through the door of their on-campus apartment.

"You scared me," Jordan admitted sleepily, willing her breath back to normal.

"Sorry," Jenna said with a cheery grin.

Her smile sent a pang of nostalgia through Jordan's heart. She missed the way things used to be—back when she actually had a full-time roommate.

"What are you up to?" Jordan asked.

"Just grabbing a dress for tonight."

"Oh yeah?" Jordan tried her best to sound enthusiastic. "Do you two have big plans?"

Jenna looked at Jordan as if she had lost her mind. "Don't you remember? Tonight is Mark's birthday."

Her tone was accusatory, but Jordan forced herself to remain calm. She offered a smile. "That's right. Tell him I said happy birthday."

"I will," Jenna said, oblivious to the fact that the world did not fully revolve around her or her boyfriend.

With that, Jenna bounded back down the hallway, disappearing into her room.

"Have a good night," Jenna called before slamming the door closed again.

"Have a good week," Jordan said softly, even though there was no longer anyone else to hear it.

Jordan let out her frustrations with a sigh. Couldn't that girl ever close a door normally? She tried to picture the friend she had known and loved for so many years, but right now all she could she muster was anger and resentment.

It wasn't the fact that Jenna had a boyfriend or a life outside of their friendship; it was the simple fact that she had disappeared. Jordan now saw her once a week or less, and her disappearance happened when Jordan needed a friend the most.

She wanted to give in and let the tears fall, but she resisted, opting instead for a workout.

Glancing at the clock, she realized she had slept longer than she intended to after returning from class. What was supposed to have been an hour-long nap had turned into three.

She shrugged. She didn't really have any plans that evening anyway, so it didn't really matter.

After her workout at the gym, she felt better. But her anger still lurked below the surface. She couldn't quite decide who she was angry with or why. All she knew was that she needed to do something.

Back at her apartment, she took a deep breath and settled onto her desk chair.

She ran through possibilities. It was a Thursday night, but there had to be something going on somewhere on campus—or at least in this town.

Her heart sank as she remembered that she would have been on a bus, headed to Oklahoma for a big game right now if her life hadn't been so unbelievably thrown off course. Feeling every bit alone as she had ever felt, she hung her head and let the tears stream down her face.

After a few minutes of giving in completely to the assault of emotion, she straightened her shoulders and wiped her eyes. She wasn't going to do this anymore. She was a fighter and a strong girl, and she was going to grab hold of her life and move forward.

With renewed determination, she pulled out her cell phone. Maybe it was a night for a new friend, she mused. Taylor's face popped into her mind, and for a moment, she got lost in remembering. Everything about Taylor was enchanting. The thought alone troubled Jordan. There had never been a point in time when she wanted to befriend someone quite as badly as she wanted to Taylor.

It was probably just the overwhelming loneliness, she assured herself. Even so, her eagerness was causing her hands to tremble slightly, and she cursed herself. If she had any shot at keeping this girl as a friend, she was going to have to play it a little cooler. No one wanted to be friends with an overeager, clingy, loner girl.

Nonetheless, if she didn't ask, she'd never know. She let out a deep breath, and had to laugh at herself. It was as if she were preparing for major surgery—not a simple text message to a girl she had only met once.

Still, she stared at the blank screen.

Hey.

Hi there.

Hello. How are you?

What's up?

She thought through her various opening lines. None of them seemed adequate.

Her phone buzzed in her hand, breaking through her thoughts and causing her to almost drop it from her grip.

It was a simple message from Taylor. *Hey new friend!*

She laughed out loud. Somehow Taylor managed to one-up her and make even that message sound cooler than it had any right to be.

I was actually just about to text you, Jordan replied. *How are you?* Her smile grew with each word she typed, until she sat there smiling like a fool.

The fact that Taylor had reached out to her meant more to her than she could put into words.

As they texted back and forth, it became obvious that neither of them had plans.

Finally, Jordan decided to make the first move. *Do you want to hang out tonight?*

Taylor's reply was instant. *Sure. What do you have in mind?*

Jordan's mind raced through possibilities. More than anything, she wanted some time to get to know this girl, but she didn't want to appear to be lame.

Deciding that renting and watching a movie, while eating pizza, might be the best way to spend some fun new friend time. She extended the invitation.

Fifteen minutes later, she heard a knock on her front door.

When she opened it, Taylor smiled and lifted up a grocery bag.

Jordan's eyebrows rose in curiosity. "What's in the bag?" she said with a laugh.

"Supplies for a girls' night," Taylor said with a shrug and a mischievous grin.

Jordan's curiosity got the best of her, and she took the bag. Inside, she found a bottle of vodka, candy, and two chick flicks.

She laughed nervously. Having never been much of a drinker, she wasn't quite sure how to respond. It made it even more intense that the preacher's daughter was the one supplying the alcohol.

"Thank you," she finally managed.

"Not what you had in mind?" Taylor asked, suddenly looking ashamed as if she had crossed a line.

Jordan weighed her response. No, it was not what she had in mind, but then again, she was no longer a basketball player. Her days of treating her body like a temple for the sake of sports had come to an end. She no longer had training sessions every day, so a few drinks wouldn't kill her.

"I'm sorry," Taylor said in response to Jordan's silence.

"Don't be sorry," Jordan said, holding up her hand to stop Taylor's apology. "I was just considering it. That's all. This will be awesome. Thank you."

A look of curiosity briefly flashed on Taylor's face, as if she wanted to know exactly the train of thought that had played through Jordan's mind. But in an instant her face was composed and she followed Jordan into the apartment.

Jordan flipped through the movies, before picking *The Ugly Truth*.

"Is this one okay?" she asked hesitantly.

Taylor nodded and offered a smile.

Jordan popped it into her DVD player, before taking a seat beside Taylor on the couch.

Out of the corner of her eye, Jordan studied the bottle of vodka. It had a little black dress on the label, and looked appealing to the eye. However, she had no real experience with alcohol, so she had no idea whether or not it would be good.

"I'm guessing you're not much of a drinker?" Taylor questioned, following Jordan's doubtful gaze.

Jordan laughed. "It's not that I'm opposed to it," she said slowly. "I just haven't ever really done much of it."

Taylor nodded, taking in the news with a bit of surprise. "I thought everyone in Kansas drank," she said, and laughed. "You definitely don't have to have any of it if you don't want to," she added.

Her words were genuine, and Jordan could easily see that there would not be any pressure. Still, she embraced the wild and fun part of her that had seemed to come alive in Taylor's presence.

"No, I'm fine," she said, her smile growing. "I think I'd actually like to try it."

She looked down to find that her hands were shaking slightly with anticipation. "I've had a few beers before," she nervously explained. "But, never alcohol. I was always too focused on sports, and I was afraid that it would ruin my performance."

"Are you sure you want to try it now?" Taylor asked.

Without waiting a second, Jordan replied, "I'd love to."

In that moment, Jordan knew that Taylor could talk her into anything—not that she would. Still, Jordan felt like Taylor's influence was strong, the pull to her magnetized.

"All right," Taylor said, amused. "Let's do it then."

With an ease of skill that told Jordan this was far from Taylor's first rodeo, Taylor spun the cap of the bottle. It came off quickly in her hand, and a smile danced on Taylor's lips before she turned the bottle upward and without even a wince took a deep swig. She handed Jordan the bottle.

Jordan willed herself to relax, but she knew for a fact that her eyes had widened significantly. She gulped back the last bit of hesitancy and took the bottle.

Mimicking what she had seen Taylor do, she put the bottle to her lips and drank. Part of her wanted to spit the alcohol out, but instead she forced it down her throat. She set the bottle down, wincing at the sting. "That was kind of rough," she said with a laugh. She was prepared for a slight teasing.

Instead, Taylor eyed her cautiously. "Are you okay?" she asked.

"I'm great," Jordan said. "In fact, I think I want to try a little bit more of that."

"Go for it," Taylor said, taking another drink before sliding the bottle back in her direction.

As Jordan tasted the bitter liquid on her tongue, a distinct image formed in her mind of throwing all caution to the wind and embracing her new life. It was as troubling as it was freeing. And at that moment she decided to let go of any guilt as well. For the time being, she would make decisions based on what she wanted to do, and she would relish her newfound freedom.

She gave Taylor a sideways glance and decided that she had found her new partner in crime.

They called and ordered a pizza. The movie had already started but it didn't matter, because both of them had seen it before and it didn't matter to Jordan especially, because she was too busy enjoying Taylor's company.

They talked incessantly throughout the first half of the movie, and by the time the pizza arrived, Jordan was feeling the effects of the alcohol. She rose to get the door and pay for the pizza, only to find that her balance was not quite what it should have been.

The realization sent her into a fit of laughter. Taylor laughed too, but stood with ease and took care of the pizza.

"How are you doing?" Taylor asked her.

"I'm feeling pretty damn good actually," Jordan said, slurring her words slightly. "I just can't believe I'm drunk with the preacher's daughter."

A look that Jordan could not decipher in her drunkenness flashed through Taylor's eyes. She wanted to know more, but was distracted by Taylor's next words.

"Well, maybe you should pace yourself a little bit." Her tone was not condescending, but still Jordan felt her defenses rise.

As if sensing the fact that she had upset Jordan, Taylor placed her hand gently on Jordan's shoulder. "I just don't want you to get sick tonight," she said reassuringly.

The move was both comforting and infuriating. Jordan didn't need anyone to take care of her. She just needed a friend.

Jordan took a breath and forced away her brief feeling of resentment. Yes, she needed a friend, and she needed to make sure she didn't scare this potential friend away so soon.

"Thank you," she managed.

Taylor laughed, easily seeing through Jordan's inner turmoil. "You're quite the fiery one, aren't you?"

The way Taylor laughed brought warmth into the room and eased Jordan's expression into a smile. "I guess so," she admitted. "Sorry about that."

"Don't be sorry," Taylor said, handing Jordan the half-empty bottle of vodka. "Have another drink and let's eat our pizza."

Throughout the night, Jordan and Taylor laughed with ease. More than once, Jordan caught herself staring into Taylor's blue eyes, contemplating whether she had ever seen such a deep and beautiful color.

She wasn't quite sure if it was jealousy or sheer awe, but she knew she was enjoying herself. Each time she stood, the alcohol made her head swim. Although it was a foreign feeling, it was also a feeling of freedom—freedom and lightness that she hadn't experienced in a long time. And she relished it.

"What are you thinking?" Taylor asked, breaking into one of the few silent moments between the two of them.

"You have beautiful eyes," Jordan blurted out before thinking.

She blushed as the words escaped her lips. Apparently, one of the effects of her drunken state was a lack of verbal filter.

Taylor smiled brightly. "Well, thank you very much. That's quite a compliment coming from such a gorgeous girl."

After briefly soaking in the compliment, Jordan decided to switch the subject. She couldn't put her finger on it, but there was something that made her oddly uncomfortable about getting compliments from Taylor. It wasn't the same as when anyone else ever complimented her.

Guys frequently called her pretty or beautiful, and so did other girls. But it seemed to mean more when Taylor said it. Chalking it up to her idolization of Taylor, she shifted in her seat.

"I'd say we've already crossed off most of the basic getting-to-know-someone questions, and there's not a lot that we haven't covered," Jordan said. "So, what's your biggest secret?"

With a deer in the headlights look, Taylor took another drink of the bottle of vodka that was now almost empty. Jordan watched as she took a deep breath.

"You don't have to answer if you don't want to," Jordan said, hoping she had not crossed the line.

"No, I'll answer," Taylor said hesitantly. "I actually trust you, which is somewhat rare for me."

"Do you have trust issues?" Jordan asked, allowing her curiosity to get the best of her.

Taylor nodded in response. "I do," she answered. "They're pretty deep, but I can see that you're genuine, you don't have bad intent."

Jordan cocked her head to the side. "You can tell that just by hanging out with me for a little while?"

"I'm not wrong, am I?" Taylor asked.

"Not at all," Jordan said, knowing that her loyalty and her genuine nature were two of her best, most praised qualities. "I'm just surprised at how well and how easily you read people."

"It comes from a long history of being burned," Taylor said, her voice suddenly sounding older somehow.

Even through the haze of alcohol, Jordan could see a deep-seated hurt shining through Taylor's expression.

"I'm sorry," Jordan said in a voice barely above a whisper. "Do you want to talk about it?"

Taylor shook her head. "No. Thank you, though. But I will answer your question."

The fact that Taylor trusted her, despite obviously having been wronged in the past, touched a special place in Jordan's heart, and she waited patiently as Taylor gathered the courage to spill her deepest secret.

"When I was in college, I was a little wild," Taylor said after a moment. "I partied a lot, and I was always looking for a fun time."

Jordan had assumed that was the case. After all, most people she knew lived it up in college.

Taylor took another drink. "Sorry," she said. "This is a little harder than I thought. I guess I just don't want you to think badly of me."

Jordan reached out and touched Taylor's hand reassuringly. "I could never think badly of you."

One of the corners of Taylor's mouth lifted in a half smile. "We'll see about that in a minute," she said playfully. "Anyway, I had a really good friend named Katie. As crazy as I thought I was, Katie was ten times crazier. She had a philosophy that she was going to try everything once, just so she didn't miss out on anything life had to offer."

Taylor took another deep breath, and for a fleeting moment Jordan wondered if she really could drop a bombshell that would change how she looked at Taylor. In reality, they didn't know each other that well. Still, she felt like she had known Taylor forever, and she hoped this confession wouldn't change that. She steeled herself as Taylor appeared to be trying to find the right words.

"It wasn't long before I adopted her outlook on life," Taylor said slowly. "I, too, started to try anything and everything."

"Like drugs?" Jordan asked, her filter failing once more.

Taylor's laugh came easier now, as if Jordan had broken up some of the tension. "Well, those too, but that's not the big secret."

Jordan nodded. "Okay, well there's no judgment here," she said with a shrug. She had plenty of friends who had experimented with recreational drug use. She occasionally worried about them, but she didn't love them any less. And she certainly wouldn't think any less of Taylor for trying something when she was younger.

"Thank you for that," Taylor said. "Like I said, I was in an experimental phase. I was trying everything, and one night, Katie wanted to try something I had never tried before. Having told myself that I wouldn't say no to any of life's experiences within reason, I was in a difficult situation. So, when she came to me and said she wanted to know what it would be like to kiss a girl, I agreed to kiss her."

Taylor paused, allowing Jordan to take in the information. It was obvious that Taylor was looking to gauge Jordan's reaction, but Jordan didn't say anything in response. She used her favorite psychological trick of waiting for someone else to fill in the silence.

It worked. Taylor seemed encouraged by Jordan's impassive face. "Well, we kissed, and then it…it turned into more."

"I have lesbian friends," Jordan said, offering a quick and nervous reply. "That doesn't bother me. I'm not like the rest of this place. I don't hate those with a different skin color, and I don't hate people who love the same sex. I have an open mind." In reality, she only knew one lesbian, but she wanted Taylor to know that she was not one to judge.

Once again, Taylor laughed, but it was filled with nervousness this time. "I'm not sure I'm a lesbian," she said. "I am just saying that I have had a relationship with a woman, and that's my big secret that no one knows."

"Okay," Jordan said. "So, do you date men as well?"

Taylor nodded. "I've dated both."

"And slept with both?" Jordan asked, unable to hide her curiosity.

"Yes."

The one-word answer sent Jordan's mind to places she had never let it wander. She had always been taught that homosexuality was wrong. It had always seemed like this was a dark world that she was forbidden to even think about, and now she was finding out that the girl she had been admiring had dabbled in that darkness.

It was as exhilarating a revelation as it was scary. She realized in that moment that her hand was still on Taylor's, and suddenly she felt as if she should move it. If she moved it, however, it might appear that she was taken aback by Taylor's confession. Keeping her hand in place, she proceeded with caution.

"Well," she said finally. "It doesn't matter to me who you've slept with. I'm just happy to have you as a friend. You're an amazing person, and I'm glad to have met you."

"Thank you for that," Taylor said. "Your turn."

The smile on Taylor's face was contagious, and Jordan found herself smiling stupidly back at her. "My turn for what?"

"Don't think you're off the hook," Taylor teased. "I want to hear your secret."

Jordan racked her brain trying to think of something. She was in the presence of someone who had truly lived her college years as one should.

"I'm kind of boring in comparison," Jordan replied. "I spent most of my years wrapped up in the sport that controlled my life. My friends were all basketball players, and I haven't really had all of those typical college experiences."

"None at all?" Taylor asked. "You haven't ever woken up and regretted anything you did the night before?"

"I probably will tomorrow, with as much as I drank tonight," Jordan admitted with a small laugh. "But, no, I guess I regret not doing some things."

"Like what?"

Jordan bit her bottom lip. "Like everything," she said.

Taylor didn't verbally respond; instead, she leaned in a little closer, as if hoping for more of an explanation.

Taking the cue, Jordan sighed. "I've never done much of anything. School and basketball kept me busy around the clock. Aside from a beer at my senior prom and a beer at a party once, I never drank before tonight. Never smoked or tried drugs. I never even had sex."

Taylor's eyes widened at her admission. "You're a virgin?"

Jordan pursed her lips and nodded. That was information she didn't readily make available to everyone. "I just kept waiting for the time to be right or the situation to be right," she said. "It just never was. I had opportunities, but I never enjoyed the situations enough to go through with it."

"That's okay," Taylor told her. "It will happen when the time is right."

Jordan shrugged. "That's the thing. Now, it's just kind of awkward. I mean, I wish I had done it sooner. At twenty-one, no one wants to hear that you're a virgin."

"Really?" Taylor's question was completely sincere. "I'd think it would be something guys liked."

She shook her head. "I've actually been dumped because of it—not because I wouldn't sleep with the guy, just because he was scared of deflowering me I guess."

"Well, when you meet the right person, they won't care," Taylor said.

Jordan silently noted that she said person instead of man, but decided not to comment on it. Later, she decided, she would play through her thoughts and figure out if she thought she could ever entertain the thought of a having a woman as a lover the way Taylor had done. For now, she was focused on getting to know Taylor on a deeper level.

Sharing lesser secrets, the hours slipped away. Finally, Jordan glanced at the clock. "It's three o'clock in the morning," she said with a laugh. Her buzz had faded slowly, and now a headache was settling in, clouding her thoughts.

"Oh wow," Taylor said. "I shouldn't be keeping you up this late. I'm sorry. I should head home."

Jordan stifled a yawn. "Normally, I'm quite the night owl. It must be the alcohol. I probably should call it a night."

"Thanks again for tonight," Taylor said as she stood. "This was great."

"Thank you," Jordan said. "I enjoyed it. I really do love hanging out with you."

"Me too," Taylor said, wrapping Jordan into a hug.

As Taylor shut the door behind her, Jordan's mind was racing in a million different directions. It was hard to wrap her mind around the fact that Taylor was not only so honest and open, but she also had a dark, wild side that enticed and enamored Jordan. She couldn't explain why she was drawn to that rebel spirit, but it called to her, beckoning her to live on the edge instead of taking life so cautiously.

The questions and musings swirled through her head, and she couldn't make sense of any of it.

As she made her way to her bedroom, she tried to process her thoughts. Suddenly, she decided that it did not really matter. Whatever Taylor's former days had held was fine. Taylor was her friend, and she was excited by that fact.

CHAPTER FOUR

With the bright sunshine glinting off the slide in the park, Kurt tried unsuccessfully to position his chemistry book so that he could read it.

Studying outside always made it a little easier in his mind, but then again it also gave him the chance to see her. He thought of her long brown hair, those green eyes, and that smile that could melt even the thickest block of ice, and suddenly he was swept into a world that had little to do with the science in the book he was supposed to be studying.

"Is that book *that* good?"

He heard Jordan's melodic voice cut through his thoughts and wondered for a moment if his daydream had been that real.

However, when she ran her fingers through his hair, mussing it up a bit, he was snapped back into reality.

"Hey," he said, turning to face her, hoping his face wasn't as red as it was hot. "Sorry, I was lost in thought."

She easily slid into the spot on the park bench beside him. "No worries," she said with a smile. "What are you up to?"

"Daily grind," he said with a playful shrug.

"Me too," she said, looking down in distaste at the bulky brace on her knee.

Following her gaze, he looked at her with sadness. "I'm so sorry, Jordan," he said. "I wish things were different for you. I know you would much rather be out on a court than spending your days here building up your knee in the park."

"It's all good," she said, waving her hand as if she were brushing off his sympathy entirely. "I'm fine and getting stronger every day."

They had talked on the surface of everything for months. Every morning, she did her physical therapy in this park, and he studied. They would briefly sit and chat and then go back to their normal routines, but as he saw the light shine on her green eyes, creating a sparkle, he knew he wanted more this time.

"How are classes?" he asked instead, chickening out. Mentally, he kicked himself.

"They're not too bad," she said with a shrug. "But then again, I'm not some kind of chemist."

She laughed and playfully closed his book, making him lose his place. He didn't even care. Her laugh was such a rich, playful sound that he got lost in it entirely.

"Would you like to go to dinner Saturday?" he blurted out. The words all came out at once, and he wasn't sure it had even made a decipherable sentence.

He looked up at her, wide-eyed, wondering why he was always so awkward around her.

She smiled. "I actually have plans Saturday," she said cautiously, and his heart fell.

"But I could on Sunday," she added.

He tried not to sound too overly excited. He had to learn to play it cool. "Awesome," he said, nodding slightly. "We can do dinner on Sunday then."

"How does Mon Amour sound?" he asked, not having to think about where he wanted to take her. He had imagined their first date too many times.

Jordan crinkled her nose and shook her head quickly. "Sounds too pretentious," she said, laughing. "How about The Grand Hog? I like barbecue as much as the next guy."

He nodded, agreeing as he would have to anything she suggested.

"Sounds great," he said with a smile. "I'll pick you up at seven."

"Works for me," she said, standing up from the bench. "I have to finish this and get to class."

"I'll see you Sunday," he called after her as she left. "I'll send you a text."

She turned halfway around to face him and offered a small wave. The move was so simple and innocent, but in the moment, she looked like a seductress. He knew he was treading a dangerous line, falling for someone who might only see him as a friend. But still, he wanted more from her. He wanted her. There was no denying it.

"I'll be looking forward to it," he called out again, feeling even more awkward than before.

With her back to him, she nodded and continued her walk and he watched her with longing, wondering what it was that made her so unique.

If he was honest with himself, it was everything. She intrigued him, baffled him, and he was looking forward to getting a chance to get to know her better.

* * *

The front door slammed shut, and as much as Janelle Wilson wanted to spring into action and ask all the questions she had, she sat and stared blankly at the wall. She felt defeated, and it seemed as if her life was slowly crumbling.

"Can I have twenty bucks?"

Her son stood in front of her. Trevor's question both infuriated her and made her even more tired than she already felt.

"I gave you money this morning," she said, her words devoid of energy.

"And I need more," he said, annoyed.

His clothes smelled like pot, and she fought the urge to scream at him. Instead, she just shook her head.

"Go find something free to do," she told him.

He stomped angrily out of the room, and she convinced herself she had done the right thing. She sighed and looked at the clock. It was time to get to the office.

She quickly gathered her things and looked down to make sure she looked presentable. Her long skirt had started to form wrinkles from where she had been sitting, and she felt frumpy in the flowered blouse she was wearing. Nonetheless, at least it appeared like she had made a decent effort at some point in the day. She was dressed as much for the part as she could manage at the moment. If business casual attire was all they required, she had met expectations. Aside from her shaking hands and incinerating stress, she looked fine to walk in and play the role of "good church lady."

She laughed nervously. It felt like she was always playing a part in which she didn't quite fit.

Taking a deep breath to clear away the negative thoughts, she got into her shiny white Suburban, noting that it looked sleeker than she would ever feel. With one last glance at the house, she saw Trevor standing near his bedroom window flipping her off. Without making it obvious, she averted her gaze. There was no sense in giving him the satisfaction of looking in his direction or acknowledging his bad behavior.

As she drove past the perfect houses in the neighborhood, she had to wonder if everyone had the same type of problems or if some of these people really did live in a picture-perfect world. They all had their manicured lawns and shiny cars, and she had to assume that deep down, they were all as unhappy as she was.

Knowing it was time to be strong, she pulled into the church parking lot and set a smile on her face. Even though it looked like the fakest thing she'd ever seen, she decided it would do.

She applied a coat of lipstick and sat staring in the mirror for a moment, steeling herself against an onslaught of emotion.

Talking to herself, she began to calmly provide a much-needed pep talk.

"Here, you are in control," she said softly. "Here you make the calls. These people have problems. You don't. Just smile, hug, and offer advice."

She pushed aside the thoughts that she was the last person who should be offering any type of life advice. Instead, she focused on the intensity of her eyes and the strength of all that she had overcome.

She gave herself a "go get 'em" nod and got out of the vehicle. Checking her watch, she realized that she still had a couple of minutes before her appointment.

Making her way into the building, she offered smiles and her usual over-the-top greetings to everyone she passed.

"Well good afternoon, Pastor Reeves," she said excitedly. In the moment, all of her nervousness had faded. It was as if she were an actress putting on a show.

The thought both exhilarated her and disgusted her, but she went with it anyway. Allowing her alter ego to come alive, she oozed confidence.

He stood up from his desk and hugged her. "Good afternoon, Janelle." Standing at almost six and a half feet tall, he towered over her, as his larger-than-life smile spread across his entire face. With his gray hair and teddy bear demeanor, she always imagined he'd make a wonderful grandpa someday, although he'd likely be the most stylish grandpa anyone ever had. As usual, he was dressed more like he was ready for a photo shoot than a day at the church office. "It's good to see you." His voice was so genuine, and for a moment she envied that. It was difficult for her to mask how she truly felt or to feign interest when she had none. "Do you have an appointment this afternoon?"

"Yes, sir," she said, glancing at her file. "Apparently a young man needs to chat about some issues."

She did her best not to indulge her gossipy side around the pastor, although it spilled out most other places. Inside, she was dying to tell Pastor Reeves that this was a college boy who had impregnated his girlfriend, a high school senior. Both attended the church, and she'd been itching to tell someone the news. She practiced restraint, having to almost bite her tongue to do so.

"Well, give him some good, sound advice," Pastor Reeves said, taking his seat again.

Nodding, she slid past him into her office.

She glanced up at the nameplate on the door and stifled a laugh. Somehow the word COUNSELOR seemed to mock her today. No, she wasn't licensed. She had gone to school and had almost completed everything to be licensed. But, in the end, she hadn't needed it. She had found her way into positions like this one for a long time, listening and helping people and skating by with the bare minimum of oversight and education. The title was nothing short of a formality, and it seemed so far from the truth today. Right now, she was the one in need of counseling.

Nonetheless, she sat behind the desk and again reviewed the young man's folder.

When he walked in, he looked like he felt about three feet tall, and she knew that this would be a rewarding case. If nothing else, she had her shit together far more than this kid did. And, maybe she could actually help him out a little bit. After all, that was the only reason people ever set foot through her door—they did so when they had nowhere else to go. She was like the last stop on the trail to rock bottom, and it appeared that this one was well on his way there. In her heart, she genuinely did want to help him, but she was having a hard time focusing today.

As he talked, she listened, drawing him out with a few questions, whether he had prayed for God's help with his substance abuse, taking notes. The whole time, she had to fight her wandering mind. There was no doubt that she was in over her head at home, but viewed from the outside, her family looked picture perfect.

She intended to keep it that way. She planned to sit down and have a serious talk with Trevor when she got home.

As the session wrapped up, she forced a smile. "It's going to be okay," she told the young man, placing a hand on his shoulder. "I'll be here for you. Remember that there's forgiveness in every situation. God has already forgiven you. Now, you just have to work on forgiving yourself and focus on being the best dad you can be to your child."

The words sounded hollow, even to her own ears, but she continued encouraging him until he was out the door. She shuffled the paperwork into a file and smoothed her shirt.

She stepped out into the main office to find Pastor Reeves waiting.

"How did it go?" he asked with a warm smile.

"It went well, I think, as a start," she said. She had learned early on in counseling to never make even tentative judgments. As much as she could think that progress was being made, someone could go off the deep end tomorrow and make her look like a joke. That was the last thing she wanted—especially here.

Here, she was a goddess. Here, she was well respected. That was more than she could say about anywhere else.

"Anything exciting happening around here?" she asked, gesturing to the church building.

"There's always something going on in a church this size," he said. "Tonight we have our young adults group meeting. It should be a good time. From what I hear, they've been getting pretty large crowds."

"That's great," Janelle commented. "Is Callie still leading that group?"

Just the mention of Callie's name brought a smile to her lips. Callie had been her little project at one point. From the time the girl was in youth group, they had met regularly for coffee. Janelle considered her a friend, but she was also proud of what she had helped foster within the girl. She had trained and mentored her, and it made Janelle happy to see her doing so well.

"She is, and she's doing a great job. Although last week my Taylor led the group and had a pretty big turnout as well."

The pride that beamed in his voice was bittersweet to Janelle. She tried to ignore her distaste for Taylor, but she couldn't do it. There was just something undefinably different about that girl, and she didn't fit in here.

"I'm glad to hear that," she said quickly. "I have to run, but I hope you have a good night."

She exited the office, replaying in her mind the way Trevor often talked about Taylor.

That girl is hot.

She's so funny.

What did Trevor really know anyway? Sure, he was a bright kid. Or, at least he had been before he had decided that his only extracurricular activities would involve "making a statement" and acting out. She sighed, but his words continued to play in her head.

She lights up a room the minute she walks into it.

I really like her. We all do.

Of course everyone liked her. She was smart, funny, friendly, and drop-dead gorgeous. But, that didn't change the fact that she didn't belong here. None of the Reeves family did, but Pastor Reeves and his wife had to be here, and she had to work for them.

Taylor was just an unnecessary added burden, and she seemed so perfect that it made Janelle's stomach turn. She was always sweeping in to seemingly save the day for some church program, and always looked flawless doing so.

But, she couldn't be that perfect. No one was, she knew that from her counseling work. Surely there was a weak spot in that girl's past. There had to be something that made her a little less perfect.

She would find out what it was.

* * *

The steam from her coffee cup rose, clouding her face and making Callie feel as if she were in a vaguely remembered Mafia movie.

"What's up?" she asked to a very agitated Janelle sitting across from her at their favorite spot to grab coffee, Bird's-Eye View Café.

Janelle slowly sipped her coffee and set the cup back down onto the table.

"I'm concerned," she said.

Callie looked at Janelle, noting that she looked aged today. The lines around her eyes seemed to have deepened, and it appeared she hadn't been sleeping well. As usual, her dark hair was perfectly styled, and she looked more put together than she would ever really be in reality. Still, she bore a ragged look on her face, as though she had just finished fighting a long, losing battle. "What are you concerned about?"

"Everything," Janelle blurted. "You and I both know that since Pastor Reeves swooped into town with that wife and daughter of his, nothing's been the same."

Callie nodded, considering all of this. Personally, she had nothing against Pastor Reeves, but she could definitely agree that his wife and daughter had pushed their way into things that were none of their business. And it was no secret that Callie didn't like Taylor; nor did Taylor like Callie. If push came to shove, there could be rough waters ahead.

"I agree," Callie said hesitantly. "But he's not the problem."

"Not at all," Janelle said quickly. "He's great, and he's maintained the size of the church, which means we're still the most prominent draw in town. Both of us have steady jobs—for now, and the church is doing well. It's just that something isn't right with that family."

"How so?"

"I mean, I think we have to keep Taylor and Donna in check or things will go south in a hurry," Janelle said matter-of-factly.

"You mean, things will be bad for us?"

"For you, for me, for all of the church staff."

"You don't think that they're going to try to get rid of some of us, do you?" Callie asked. She hated Taylor for reasons of her own, but she'd not quite put the figures together that Taylor might have some influence on her job. Pastor Reeves usually seemed quite content to let matters of personal conflicts take care of themselves, while he let his staff go about their business.

Janelle shrugged. "I don't think it would come to that, but you've seen the way they look at us. They act like they're better than we are."

"I said that just the other day." Callie sat up straighter in her chair. "The guys all told me it was all in my head. But I guess it's not just me."

"No," said Janelle, shaking her head. "I've seen it too."

They sipped their coffee in silence. Janelle changed the subject. "Anyway, I've had enough of talking about them," she said. "How is the group?"

Callie considered the question. "I'm not sure, honestly," she answered. "There are times when it's great, but lately, even though numbers are up, it just feels like things are off."

"What do you mean?"

"I just mean that I think we could have some problems around the corner," she said. "Basically, it all boils down to Taylor again. If she wants to take over, I see no reason why Pastor Reeves wouldn't just let her do it. She is his daughter, and he trusts her. I'm just an outsider to him, even though I've been here for much longer."

"Does she act like she wants to?" Janelle asked.

It was Callie's turn to shrug. "I'm not sure. She apparently had a good turnout the other night, even got some new people there."

"What new people?"

"A couple of college guys and one girl who everyone says used to play on the basketball team over at the university," Callie said.

"Basketball player?" Janelle asked. "Don't tell me Jordan Weston showed up?"

"I think that was her name." Callie asked, "How do you know her?"

"I'm an old friend of her mom's. Jordan's mom has been pushing her to come check out the group for months, but apparently she hadn't been showing any interest. I talked to her mom a while back, and she said she was still trying to talk her into going."

"Well, she showed up last week and again this week," Callie said. "She was sickeningly glued to Taylor's side this time. It was like she was an old friend of Taylor's, so I didn't pay much attention.

"According to everyone who was there last week, the night Taylor led went well," Callie continued. "We got the people back again this week, so I just feel like the pressure is on me to keep performance high."

Janelle's eyes narrowed. "Don't you worry," she said with a low voice. "When Taylor falls off her mighty pedestal, which she will, we'll put her in her place, and then you won't even have to think twice about her snatching your group out from under your nose. Even her daddy's good name won't be able keep her in a high position."

Something inside Callie came alive. She hated to give rein to the retaliatory part of her soul, but the temptation was just too great. She felt the neutral expression on her face give way to a devious smile.

"We'll put her back in her place, and hopefully she'll just go home," she said.

Together, they sat and drank coffee into the night, discussing everything and everybody as usual. After going through a list of gossip items she had cleverly titled as "prayer requests," she finally looked at the clock.

"I should probably go," she said. "But, thanks for reassuring me that this is all going to be okay. We'll get through it together."

Callie couldn't quite interpret the look in Janelle's eyes. It could have been any number of emotions—ranging from a desire to seek revenge to sadness. Either way, she was glad to have Janelle on her side. There was no doubt that Janelle had faced a number of nemeses in her day, and that she somehow always came out on the other side, while her opponents suffered greatly.

As she got into her car, she couldn't help but smile at the thought of Taylor's perfect persona being destroyed at Janelle's hand. It would be sincerely satisfying to have her knocked off her high-and-mighty perch where she could no longer sit on top of the world.

Still, Callie knew she had to be careful. Taylor was her daddy's little girl, and if Callie didn't at least pretend to like her, there was no doubt whose side the good pastor would take.

She replayed the first night she had attempted to befriend Taylor. It had been an insincere act of self-preservation. Keep your friends close and your enemies closer. Right away, she had dubbed Taylor as an enemy.

Anyone whose beauty and personality shone brighter than her own was an enemy in this small town. She refused to share the spotlight with anybody, but Taylor had been making that a difficult task, so she had suggested they hang out after work.

They'd coexisted in a friendly manner throughout the night until Callie started asking personal questions.

Taylor refused to answer most of them, disguising her discomfort with what she obviously hoped were good-natured laughs. Finally, when Callie continued to press, Taylor had flat-out said that she wasn't sure she could trust anyone here, and she wasn't one to make close friends easily.

"No offense, I just don't trust many people," Taylor had said.

Letting the memory steep, Callie let out a sigh.

"No offense, Taylor Reeves, but you're a bitch," she said aloud in her car.

If that girl wanted a reason not to trust, Callie could sure as hell give her one. And, given the right situation, she would do just that. For now, she would just bide her time and let Janelle do most of the dirty work.

Then, eventually she would watch as Taylor fell from grace. It would be glorious, and she could have her life back as undisputed queen bee.

CHAPTER FIVE

"Listen to this one," Taylor said, bringing up a music video from the nineties on YouTube for Jordan.

Jordan bobbed her head along with the beat and then started laughing when she heard the words.

"What is this?" she asked.

"Guttermouth," Taylor said with a laugh. "It's long before your time, little one."

"I'm not so little," Jordan retorted, moving her body in dancing rhythm. "In case you haven't noticed, I look you in the eye."

Taylor nodded. "You sure do, but you're also pretty damn young."

"Old enough to know better, young enough not to care," Jordan said, flopping down on the bed beside her.

Taylor laughed with ease and relished the comfort of the situation. For having known each other only a week, they had fallen into an easy friendship.

Surprisingly, they had spent almost every day together, and had been through secrets, girl talk, dreams, future plans, and fears. It was comforting to Taylor, but also quite frightening. It had been a long time since she had opened up to someone on this level, and it never ended well for her. More often than not, Taylor had learned that opening up to someone usually led to being burned and getting hurt or doing the hurting herself when her father was reassigned to a new church. Throughout her life, broken trust was a common theme.

She kept waiting for the ball to drop, but she was enjoying herself so much that she had decided to just let it happen this time. Come what may, she was immersing herself in this friendship with Jordan Weston, and it was a welcome break from her typical closed-off approach.

Emerging from her thoughts, she realized that Jordan was staring at her inquisitively.

"What's up?" Taylor asked.

"I was just thinking how happy I am to have a friend like you," Jordan said.

"I would have to say the feeling is mutual."

"And..." Jordan let her voice trail off to build suspense. "I was wondering if you would be willing to help me pick out an outfit for tonight."

"What's happening tonight?" Taylor asked.

"I think I have a date," Jordan said slowly.

"You think?" Taylor ignored the flip-flop of her heart at Jordan's confession, and remained poised.

Jordan shrugged and scrunched up her face. "I mean, this guy has been a friend of mine for a while, and I know he likes me. He asked me to dinner."

"So, he likes you," Taylor said. "But, do you like him?"

Her head to one side, Jordan appeared to be fully contemplating the situation. "He's like a bro," she said with a light laugh. "You know, he's that guy I talk to every day about nothing. Our conversations are never really substantial. We chat about sports, the weather, our classes, and my physical therapy.

It's never deeper than that, but his eyes linger far too long to be comfortable sometimes. He does the awkward thing where he occasionally has conversations with my breasts, and he stutters sometimes out of nervousness. I know he likes me. He's given plenty of hints before, and now he asked me out. I'm pretty positive it's a date."

Taylor laughed again. This girl was hilarious even when she didn't really mean to be. "Right, but how do you feel about him?"

"I'm not sure," she admitted. "I don't think I'm crazy about him, but I'll give it a shot. I might as well. I never go on dates, and I usually find an excuse when someone asks me to go out with them. My mom is always telling me that I don't give anyone a chance."

"You're too young for your mom to be putting that kind of pressure on you."

"Maybe I am," Jordan said, considering the thought. "But she is kind of right, you know? I just haven't been into dating. I didn't ever really have the time, and when I did, I lost interest pretty quickly."

"Is that why you're a virgin?" Taylor teased.

Jordan allowed her mouth to drop open in pretend shock. "Miss Reeves, I'm surprised at your candor," she said in a proper tone.

They laughed, before Jordan broke into a grin ear to ear. "Yeah, that's probably why," she admitted. "If I'm not interested, how am I supposed to sleep with anyone?"

"You make a good point," Taylor conceded. "But are you telling me there's never been anyone who's sparked your interest?"

"Not in a sexual way, I don't think."

Jordan had been more than willing to deepen conversations to this point, so Taylor decided to take the conversation one step further.

"So, there's never been anyone you fantasize about? You don't have special thoughts when you take care of yourself?"

Jordan's eyes widened, and Taylor's amusement grew.

"Sorry," she said with a smile. "I figured it was time to put you on the spot for a change."

Jordan blushed and looked down for a moment.

"I just don't think I've ever shared those conversations with anyone," she said. "I don't really have anyone in particular I think about when I do that."

Taylor laughed, trying to ease Jordan back into comfort. "Don't think too much about it," she said. "We'll get on an easier topic. Tell me more about this guy." Taylor wanted to linger on the subject in her mind, to figure out what it was that made this girl tick, but she let it go for the time being.

"His name is Kurt," Jordan said quickly, obviously thankful to no longer be talking about her fantasies. "He's a science geek, but he's fairly attractive." She continued to report random facts about Kurt. "He's really nice, and he's a senior in college. I think he wants to go into medicine. He likes sports, but he always talks about video games."

"You sound like you're making a grocery list," Taylor teased. "That's definitely not how you would describe someone you're into."

"I don't know if I'm into him," she said. "That's the problem. I never really know."

"Well, what's your type?" Taylor asked, smiling to herself as she watched Jordan's every move. She talked animatedly with her hands, and her expressions seemed to always give away her true feelings. From her little nose crinkles to the way her smile would actually light up her eyes when it was genuine, the girl could entertain Taylor all day with just a simple story.

Her long lean body swayed as she slowly moved her head from side to side, as she seemed to consider the question, and Taylor was mesmerized with every movement.

"I don't think I have a type," Jordan said. "There are actually very few guys I find myself attracted to at all. I guess I don't really notice guys most of the time."

"That's not a bad thing," Taylor said. "You're just picky." Even as she said the words, she broke into a smile. It was just too much fun to tease Jordan a little bit and watch her get flustered.

"I'm not picky. I just want someone who gives me butterflies. I want someone to take my breath away. I don't want a love I can live with. I want a love I can't live without."

"Well said," Taylor noted, genuinely impressed. "I think you'll know when you find that person."

Jordan's smile grew. "I think I will too, but for now, I'll give people a chance. Besides, if I go on a date or two, maybe my mom will get off my back a little."

"Why is she so worried about it? I mean, you're gorgeous, you're smart, and you're going places. You're going to find someone incredible."

"I think she's worried I'm either going to become the cat lady, a nun, or a lesbian," Jordan joked.

"I don't think you're in any danger of becoming any of those things," Taylor said.

"We shall see," Jordan said, cocking her head to the side and winking.

The move almost made Taylor come undone. This girl had no idea how seductive she was without even trying. Silently, Taylor chastised herself. She was going to have to put those thoughts aside, and she'd successfully done so at every turn until Jordan went and did something like this.

"So are you excited about your date?" Taylor asked, bringing the conversation back to its starting point.

"I think so," Jordan said. "It's bound to be better than some of my previous dates."

"Tell me about them," Taylor said, turning to lie on her side so she could face Jordan.

"Let's just say that if he doesn't show up drunk, try to take off my clothes at the restaurant, or pretend he lost his wallet, it'll be the best college date I've had so far."

Taylor laughed, and Jordan's lips turned up into a grin, making her dimple even more noticeable.

"Have they all been that bad?"

"They have," Jordan said with a telling wince. "But, maybe this one will be different."

It was amusing to Taylor that she sounded almost analytical about it. There was none of the typical girl musing about her upcoming date. There was no starriness about her tone. She was grounded, and her heart was not about to be senselessly smashed into pieces by anyone.

For a moment Taylor envied that, but then she remembered how incredible it felt to fall in love. It was worth all the pain.

"Give it a chance," Taylor told her, speaking from experience. "If it's not great, don't push it, but you never know till you try. Sometimes love comes in unexpected places."

With a nod, Jordan considered the words. "I'll give him a chance," she said, standing and leaving her place on the bed. "Let's look at my options."

Taylor rolled over again, enjoying a rare moment of laziness. "Show me," she said, stacking a pillow behind her head to make her view better.

One by one, Jordan held up outfits. All of them would undoubtedly look fantastic, and Taylor imagined her wearing each one. She considered the options carefully, wanting Jordan to look her best, in hopes that she might have the time of her life on this date with science nerd, Kurt.

"The tight jeans with the red slouch top," Taylor instructed after Jordan had finished.

"You think so?" Jordan questioned.

"I do," Taylor said. She was sold on it from the second Jordan held it up, and decided she would make her case for the outfit.

"Wear the tight jeans, because they show off your incredible body," she said. "Wear the red slouch because it also shows off your curves, but it still showcases your toned arms. Also, red looks incredible on you. It makes your dark hair shine and your green eyes come to life."

A look that was a mix between astonishment and gratitude crossed over Jordan's face.

"What's wrong?" Taylor asked.

Jordan shook her head. "Nothing," she said. "It's just that I'm pretty sure I've never gotten such an in-depth compliment, so full of detail. Thank you."

Taylor breathed a sigh of relief at the knowledge that Jordan's reaction was to be flattered and not offended or scared.

"You're very welcome," she said softly.

A comfortable silence fell over the room as Jordan dressed, did her makeup and chose the right jewelry to pair with the outfit.

"What time is your date?" Taylor asked, glancing at the clock.

"He should be here at five thirty," Jordan replied. "It's five now. How do I look?"

"You look great," Taylor assured her. "I'm going to go now so you can finish."

"Okay," Jordan said, coming over to wrap Taylor into a hug. "You really are incredible. Thank you for everything."

"It's always my pleasure," Taylor said, returning the hug. "Now, you go out and have a blast. Give him a shot, and let me know how it goes after the date."

Jordan smiled, suddenly looking like the young college girl that she was. It made Taylor happy to see her like that instead of looking like she had the weight of the world on her shoulders. She sincerely hoped that the date went well and that maybe Kurt could make Jordan that happy all the time.

"I'll text you," Jordan called out after her.

"Talk to you later," Taylor replied. "Have fun!"

She was almost out the door when Jordan came running up from behind her. "Wait," she said.

"What's up?" Taylor asked, half turning back to her.

"What are you doing later tonight?" Jordan asked.

"I'm not sure," she said. "Why? You want me to attend your date and give you a thumbs-up or thumbs-down to see if I approve?"

They both laughed at her joke, and Taylor hoped it actually was a joke. She wasn't sure she could truly give approval for this guy unless he made Jordan insanely happy.

"Would you like to come over and have a post-date wrap-up?" Jordan asked with a silly look on her face that made Taylor smile. "I promise it will be fun."

"Sounds fun," Taylor said. "But, let's see how the date goes. You may be out late if it goes well. Just text me when you're done and we'll make a plan from there."

"Okay," Jordan agreed, hugging her one last time. "I doubt I'll be out late. That's not really my style."

Taylor shrugged and winked. On the way to her truck, she decided to actually spend an evening at home, alone, for the first time all week. Aside from the one night she had gone out with some people from the church, she had either been at Jordan's house, or Jordan had been at hers.

Her presence was obviously starting to annoy Jordan's roommate, who scowled at Taylor every time she laid eyes on her, but the roommate was rarely there anyway. Taylor had offered multiple times for both of them to just hang out at her own house if that made the situation easier for Jordan, but Jordan didn't seem to care.

"You're my friend, and I want you here," Jordan had told her. "If she doesn't, it doesn't really matter. She practically lives elsewhere anyway. This is my place, and you're the one I want to hang out with here. You are always welcome here."

The words still made her laugh as she replayed them. Things were so black and white with Jordan, and she adamantly pursued what she wanted until she had her way. She was a stubborn girl.

She noticed that the light on her phone was blinking. Her eyes widened as she saw that she had six missed calls and five text messages—all from her mom. She sighed. If nothing else, her mother was persistent.

She read through each of them quickly. Apparently, she was not having a relaxing evening at home; instead, she was being included in a dinner with her family and a special guest.

She rolled her eyes at the words *special guest*. It didn't take a genius to figure out that her mother was up to her old matchmaking schemes.

Shaking her head, she could hear it all now.

He's such a good catch, honey. Strong in faith, well off, funny, and as handsome as they come.

In each town she had lived in, her mother had tried to set her up on dates at least once. It never went well, and although her mom had great taste, the guy was never what interested Taylor at the time.

Maybe this time would be different. But she doubted it. Honestly, she wasn't quite sure what she wanted at the moment, but she had a feeling her mom had even less of a clue. There had been times in her past when a good, strong man was exactly what she had wanted. This was not one of those times. Right now, she wanted someone who was completely off limits—someone with bright green eyes and a smile that damn near brought her to her knees.

With that out of the question, she figured she would give this a try. Perhaps, even though it had never happened before, her mother really did know what was best. If nothing else, maybe it would help her keep her focus where it belonged.

She went home and changed her clothes. The entire time, her mind kept wandering back to the conversation she had with Jordan about how Jordan never felt that attracted to the people she dated.

She couldn't help but think back to when she thought the same thing. There was little doubt in her mind that Jordan's reasons were different than hers, because hers had stemmed from her repressed desires.

The minute she had given in to what she really wanted in a partner, she had found attraction like she had never known. In a rare moment of reflection, she let the memories wash back over her and take her away to a slightly simpler time.

Remembering the sheer lust she had felt and Katie's long hair tangling with her own as they kissed, she felt herself shiver. She never missed Katie; nor would she ever. But there was something so passionate about the innocent love they had shared that she knew its memory would always be with her.

Katie had opened her eyes to a new world, but their relationship had also brought on its share of doubts and self-questioning that had threatened to tear her apart in the years that followed. She was, for better or for worse, the daughter of a pastor. Her thoughts shifted back to Jordan, and she hoped she never had to doubt herself in that way.

Jordan was a girl with everything going for her, and Taylor never wanted her to have reason to doubt it. If she could do anything as her friend, she would make sure Jordan knew how incredible she was.

As she put the finishing touches on her makeup, she stared into the mirror. It was suddenly strange to look into the mirror the same way she did every day and to see a new face there.

For some reason, she looked older today. Maybe it was the formation of fine lines by her eyes. Then again, it could just be the fact that she looked older after hanging out with such a young woman lately.

She thought about all the life events and dreams that Jordan had ahead of her, and she felt a bittersweet melancholy. She was not unhappy with her life, but she had to admit that a part of her missed the freedom and the mindset that life was full of possibility that came with early adulthood.

With one final look in the mirror, she sighed.

"That's as good as it's going to get today," she said to herself before heading out the door.

Once she arrived at her parents' house for dinner, she was thankful to see that their "special guest" had not yet arrived.

"There's my girl," her dad bellowed from down the hallway.

His deep voice brought a smile to her face. It was the voice that had read her stories as a child and comforted her all of her life. As much as they had moved around, his voice was one of the few things that had remained the same in her ever-changing world. It was one of the things that brought her the most comfort, even to this day.

"Hey, Dad," she said, falling easily into his embrace.

"It seems like we haven't seen you in a while," he noted, taking a step back to look at her. "But, you look just as beautiful as always."

"Thank you," she said, ignoring his comment about not seeing her. "You look good too, Dad. I like the spiky cut," she said, reaching up to pat his head.

"You know I like to keep in style," he said with a laugh.

She laughed with him. It was true. There was no doubt her father's vainness would always manifest in only the best and latest in fashion and hairstyles. Even for a family dinner, he was dressed to the nines in dark jeans and a pressed bright green Ralph Lauren button-down shirt. Always the eccentric one, he had cut his hair short enough to resemble a spikier cut, typically worn by thirty-somethings or younger.

She bypassed him, unable to carry on casual conversation when she knew it would turn into an interrogation. She was almost thirty, and she had to form lines of separation at times. Otherwise, they got slightly clingy.

"Where's Mom?" she asked.

"In the kitchen, cooking up a feast," he said with a smile. His eyes twinkled as if there was a big surprise that he wasn't telling her.

"I know that Mom is playing matchmaker," she said dryly. "You don't have to pretend like you don't know it, too."

He gave her a look of mock surprise. "I know no such thing," he said teasingly. Then, he shrugged. "Okay, I do know, and I think you'll like him."

She shook her head. "I'll keep an open mind," she told him. "That's all I can promise."

"Good enough," he said, turning to go into the kitchen.

Taylor followed him, and her mom looked up at her. "Sweetheart," she gasped. "You look beautiful."

"Thanks, Mom," Taylor said. She was thankful for the comment, but her mom's enthusiasm made her a little nervous. She looked down at her outfit and knew that they were exaggerating with their compliments. She hadn't put that much effort into the evening, so that must mean that they were simply hoping their guest didn't notice.

Even her mom had outdone her, yet again. Always one to concentrate too heavily on appearances, her hair was highlighted again, and recently. The platinum color masked her age, as did her mother's designer jeans and fitted top. She looked like a sitcom cougar, Taylor noted. With one more glance down at her own outfit, she felt out of place and suddenly uneasy.

"Who exactly did you invite to dinner tonight?" she asked.

"It's a surprise," her mom said.

If there was one thing Donna Reeves was good at, it was carrying out grand surprises. But, this was one area where Taylor felt more details would give her a fighting chance.

"Shouldn't I know who it is, so I can be prepared to meet him?" Taylor asked, careful to keep her tone from sounding defensive or irritated.

Donna's smile grew. "Don't worry about it," she said.

"Mom, come on," she said, a little more sternly. "Who is it? At least tell me about him, so I don't act like a complete fool when he gets here."

A look of slight concern passed over Donna's face as if she was trying to figure out all the possible ways her daughter could come across as a fool. It was obvious she didn't like the thought.

"Fine," she said, drying her hands on a dish towel. "He's a lawyer, and he just started going to our church. He came to your father's Bible study for the first time a couple of weeks ago, and he's very attractive."

"Okay," Taylor said, nodding and taking it all in. "Do I get a name? Age? Anything else?"

Her mother considered the question, and Taylor noted that her date for the evening was obviously her mom's type. He was going to be nothing like the men she preferred to date, when she dated men. Nonetheless, she would do exactly as she had always been taught. She would be polite, she would smile, she would laugh at his jokes, and she would behave as a good preacher's daughter ought to behave.

On the inside, she was already screaming. Having spent her entire life under the microscope and on display, she hated having to act that way at home. But she would get through it as she always did. It was the same dull and tired routine.

"You'll get more information soon enough," Donna said, continuing to cook. She glanced at the clock. "He should be here in ten minutes, anyway, so you don't have to wait too long."

"I think you'll like him, too, for what that's worth," her dad said from the opposite side of the kitchen. "He's a great young man—just the type of guy who would make a good son-in-law."

"Comments like that are off limits once he gets here, understand?" Taylor asked in mock seriousness. "We can't have people in this town going around and spreading rumors that the Reeves family believes in arranged marriages."

Both of her parents laughed, and she felt herself relax—slightly.

A knock on the front door made her stiffen again.

"He's early," Donna said with a grin. "That's a good sign. We all appreciate being prompt."

"I'll get it," her dad said, jumping up from his chair.

Her parents' excitement made her head swim. It was as if they felt that she would never find anyone, and they were chomping at the bit to marry her off to anyone who might fit the bill of happily ever after.

The thought made her stomach dip slightly. She was pretty sure her definition of happily ever after varied quite a distance from theirs, but at the moment she didn't have any other interesting dating prospects. Might as well give it a try.

Then one of the most attractive men she had seen in Kansas walked into the living room, looking like he had stepped from the pages of a magazine. Even through his businesslike clothing Taylor could tell his body was chiseled like that of a Greek god. His wavy, thick, dark hair, broad shoulders, and brown eyes, combined with his olive skin, made him look like a male model.

"Hello," he said, nodding in her direction. "I'm Luke."

"I'm Taylor," she replied, shaking his hand.

"It's very nice to meet you," he said.

"Nice to meet you too," she offered.

It was clear he had tried to disguise the move, but she saw his eyes widen slightly as he looked her up and down. She felt more than a little uncomfortable under his gaze. It was less about the looking. Most men looked, but it was the fact that he was looking while she was in the room with her parents. Worse yet, she didn't want him to look. The thought of his interest was enough to make her stomach turn.

While he had every attribute that should make him the most eligible bachelor in the state, she felt nothing when she looked at him. He was too put together, too pretty, too perfect. It was as if he were polished to be on display at a museum. He would have fit perfectly into a pastor's family, looking every bit the part. In a nutshell, he was everything her mother wanted her to find—and nothing she herself wanted to find.

As they all made their way into the dining room, she tried to place her finger on exactly what it was she did want to find.

It all came together in one word. *Passion.* Usually, that meant imperfection and a little craziness, but she wanted to find someone she was absolutely crazy about—someone she could not deny, even if she wanted to do so. She didn't want comfort or perfection; she wanted someone who drove her crazy in all the best ways.

This man sitting across from her was the farthest thing from her mind, but she did her best to practice politeness anyway. After all, it was not his fault that he had been set up on a blind date by an overzealous pastor and his wife. He didn't seem to mind the concept, though. It was as if he had wanted to be put on the market and had willingly accepted the challenge of dating the preacher's daughter. In Taylor's mind, that made him almost as sick as her parents were over the whole concept.

They made small talk about how he had lived in Kansas for all of his life—except for his college career. Taylor struggled to remain interested and engaged, but it didn't really matter if she did. Her parents were keeping the conversation going at a quick flow, asking questions one after the other. He was easygoing enough and didn't seem to mind the barrage of questions. Obviously, he was pleased with himself and didn't mind sharing. The arrogance was a little too thick for Taylor to stand, but she managed to sit through it all with a smile, tuning in when he talked about his career, just in case she was quizzed on it later.

"I mainly practice family law cases," he said, his chest puffing out as he talked. Taylor couldn't help but wonder if he knew how transparent he looked. "I feel like people in tough situations need a champion."

Had he really just called himself a champion as if no one would think that odd? She fought to keep herself from shaking her head, and looked over to see her parents hanging on every word he said.

"Divorces and custody battles are dirty, and people just need someone strong to turn to in those times," he continued.

She wished that she had a drink to slam to get through this, but kept listening as he continued to babble. There was no doubt he was successful as a lawyer. He could talk and talk. He probably bored the other side, until they just gave up.

By the time dinner was over, she felt like she could have written a book about Luke Carter, but she figured it would have been so dry and boring that no one would have even bothered to pick it up off the shelves. Had she written it, she would have titled it *The Life and Times of a True Champion*, just for satirical purposes.

Once conversation had died down, Taylor stood and helped her mom clear the table. Thankfully, Luke and her father went to go talk baseball in the other room.

"What do you think?" her mom asked, nudging her in the side.

Taylor sighed. She didn't want to get into this argument again. She had heard it all before. She wasn't putting herself out there enough, and she wasn't getting any younger. Her mother was always quick to remind her that her clock was ticking, and if she didn't settle down soon she was going to miss out on the opportunity to complete her life by having a husband and children.

"He was nice," she finally managed.

"Nice?" Donna questioned. "I was hoping more along the lines of hot, amazing or intriguing."

Taylor laughed. "I'm sure he's all of those things, Mom. I'm just not sure he's a good fit for me."

"Why not?" her mother asked, thumping down a pan. She'd gone to a lot of trouble with this dinner and her irritation was rising.

"I don't know," she said, shrugging. She wanted to scream that he was just too damn perfect but not at all perfect for her. Instead, she decided to appease her mother. "Let's just play it by ear, okay? If he asks me on a date, I'll go. If not, we'll move on without a word."

Donna looked like she might protest, but instead, she nodded. "Deal."

Taylor smiled. It was very rare for her mother to concede on anything, let it go without further cross-examination. Perhaps she should go buy a lottery ticket, because it looked like luck was in her favor today. She finished washing and drying the dishes, while her mother hummed and helped.

She had felt her phone vibrating a couple of times throughout dinner and she reached into her back pocket to see what was going on.

There was a missed call from Jordan and two text messages. *Hey. Call me when you get this.*

An hour later, the next one read: *I'm sure you're busy, but, if you still want to come over tonight, you should.*

She looked at the time. Jordan's dinner date should still be going, or at the very least should have just ended. She hoped it hadn't gone badly.

"What's wrong?" Donna asked.

Taylor shook her head. "Nothing is wrong, Mom. I just have a friend that needs some help. Do you mind if I head out now?"

The disappointment on her mom's face was evident, but she nodded anyway. "Go ahead," she said reluctantly.

"Thank you for that wonderful dinner," she said, giving her a hug. "I'll be over soon."

To keep her mom at least somewhat appeased, she also went into the living room to hug her father and thank Luke for coming over to dinner. Whether he was disappointed or not she could not read in his bland, perfect, lawyerly features. She glanced back into the kitchen where Donna was grinning like a love-struck teenager. It might be some consolation that she'd have Luke to herself for as long as he chose to remain.

Shaking her head in a mix of amusement and irritation, she made her way to her car. Then hit the callback button.

After three rings, Jordan picked up the phone.

"Hello?" she said, her voice suddenly sounding smaller than it had been earlier.

"What's wrong?" Taylor asked, already knowing enough about Jordan to intuit that she was upset.

"Nothing really," Jordan said. "What have you been up to?"

"I got sucked into dinner at my parents' house, but I'll tell you all about that later," Taylor said. "Are you sure you're okay?"

"I don't know," Jordan said. "Nothing is wrong. I'm just having a bad night."

"Do you still want me to come over?" Taylor asked.

"I'd love that."

"Good," Taylor said with a smile. "Ben, Jerry, and I will be there in a little bit."

CHAPTER SIX

Biting her nails, Jordan paced anxiously by the doorway. When she finally heard Taylor's car drive up, she quickly sat on the couch. She didn't want to appear like she had been desperately waiting for company.

The thought made her sick to her stomach. When had she become the girl who depended on someone else to make her feel better? She let out a sigh that became more of a sigh of relief as she heard the knock on the door.

"Come in," Jordan called, hoping she didn't look too keyed up from the night's events. She tried to straighten her rumpled shirt.

The door opened slowly, and she saw Kurt awkwardly lean his head in the doorway.

"Oh, hi," she said in surprise.

"Expecting someone else?" Kurt asked, picking up on her tone.

She nodded. "I have a friend coming over in a few minutes."

She spoke the words hoping that he would take the hint and move on without issue.

"Okay," he said, hanging his head a bit. "I won't take too much of your time. I just wanted to apologize for tonight—for whatever went wrong tonight."

Jordan tried to still her emotions, but it was like trying to tame fireflies. There was no question that she was simply a wreck tonight.

"Was it my joke about your name being a type of gun?" he asked awkwardly.

Jordan laughed slightly. "No, it wasn't," she said. "But, for future reference that's a Smith and Wesson you were referring to—not Weston."

His face turned beet red, and he looked away for a moment. Jordan's feelings of guilt welled up inside of her, and she wanted to comfort him—but more than anything, she wanted him to go away and leave her to think through everything that was happening.

She managed a smile, but even she knew that it didn't quite reach her eyes and looked far too fake. "You didn't do anything wrong," she said as she tried her best to comfort him. "I'm just having a bad day, and I think we would be better off as friends."

"I'm sorry I tried to push that limit," he said. "I hope you will still be my friend, at least."

"Of course," she said. She felt like she should go hug him, but that was the last thing she wanted to do at the moment. Instead, she sat on the couch, hugging her knees.

In the awkward silence, she could plainly see the disappointment on his face, but there was nothing she could do to change it. She knew that much now. There was no way she could force herself to have feelings for him, even if she wanted to—and she did not.

"Thanks for dinner," she said, filling the expansive silence. "I'll see you at the park this week."

He pursed his lips and nodded. "Sounds good," he said.

There was a brief pause, and he looked like he might explode if he didn't speak the words that threatened to come out of his mouth.

"So, there is no chance of us ever being more than friends?"

The pained look on his face was almost enough to make Jordan agree to a second date, but she just could not stand to lead him on, and she honestly did not know if she would survive another date with Kurt.

She shook her head. "I'm sorry. You're really great. I just think that we are much better off as friends."

"Okay," he said, forcing a sad smile. "Thanks again for giving it a shot. Have a good night."

With an uncomfortable wave, she sent him on his way. As the door closed behind him, she fought back tears. For years, she had lived with her illusions, and the truth had come crashing through in glaringly obvious fashion tonight.

And, she feared it was a truth she could not live with, even if she wanted to.

Another knock at the door sent a shot of hope through her body.

"Come in," she called, hoping that there were no more surprise visitors for the evening.

Relief flooded her when she saw Taylor step through the door with a bright smile. That smile could make just about anything better as far as Jordan was concerned. Its contagious nature spread throughout the room and put Jordan slightly at ease.

After taking one look at her Taylor asked, "What's wrong?"

The compassion was too much, and Jordan felt tears sting the corners of her eyes. She shook her head, waiting for composure to be able to form words.

Taylor set the shopping bag on the coffee table and moved to Jordan's side on the sofa. Taking her in her arms, she kissed the top of Jordan's head and held her close.

"What happened?" Taylor's voice was laden with concern. "Did that bastard do something to you?"

Jordan shook her head, and although she didn't want to leave the comfort of Taylor's arms, she brushed away her tears and moved away to look her in the eyes.

"No," she said. "He didn't. I'm sorry. I'm just a mess tonight."

"Tell me what's going on, please," Taylor said.

The genuine concern in her eyes burned intensely, and Jordan was unsure how to deal with such a steadfast and attentive friend. Most of her friends were pretty flaky and ran at the sight of human emotion. Now, she had someone begging her to open up and talk about her problems.

"I just have a lot to figure out," Jordan finally admitted. "And tonight did not help in any way. In fact, I think I'm more confused now than I've ever been."

"There's nothing wrong with a little confusion," Taylor said as she stood to grab two spoons from Jordan's silverware drawer.

Jordan noted how she navigated the kitchen with ease, as if she had been a lifelong friend. She found comfort in the notion.

"Confusion allows for self-discovery, and that's all a part of growing up and becoming who you are," Taylor said. "It's healthy and normal. What has you so confused?"

"Life, I guess," Jordan said with a sad laugh and a shrug as she took the spoon that Taylor handed her.

"Any specific parts of life?" Taylor inquired gently.

Jordan took a deep breath. She felt safe here. She had never had a safe space or a friend with whom she could share everything on her mind.

To get what you've never had, you have to do what you've never done. The words played through her mind, and she decided to go for it.

"Love," she said, her voice no longer timid. "The thing is, tonight, I felt nothing. It was unnecessarily awkward—not even that fun, first date kind of awkward. It was just awkward and painful, and there was nothing to talk about. Halfway through dinner, I realized that I was just staring at him hoping to feel some sort of attraction. But when he reached for my hand, all I could think about was the fact that his palms were probably sweaty, so I pulled away from him.

"I felt nothing for him. There was zero attraction, and that's not uncommon for me. I don't feel that attraction to anyone I date, and I long for it. I mean, I feel it at times when I'm thinking about situations in my head, but I don't have it with anyone I date."

Taylor listened, opening a pint of Cherry Garcia. She placed it into Jordan's hand and patted her on the shoulder.

"That's okay, Jordan," she said sweetly. "You can't make yourself feel things that you don't. If it's not there, it's just not."

"I appreciate you not trying to appease me by telling me that I'll find the right one or urging me to give it another shot," Jordan said. "I'm sick of hearing that."

"You and me both," Taylor laughed, taking a spoonful of the ice cream and popping it into her mouth.

"This is really good, by the way," Jordan said, pointing to the container.

Taylor nodded. "It has magical powers for making bad nights better."

They both ate in silence as Taylor gave Jordan the chance to process her thoughts. Taylor was a good listener, and allowed the silence to grow. Finally, Jordan continued. "The thing is, I want to be a normal twenty-something. I want to want to date. I want to have sex. I want to feel that attraction. I just don't." She helped herself to another bite of the ice cream, noting just how much easier it made this discussion.

"I just don't know if I will ever feel that attraction," Jordan continued. "I want to. I just never do. Tonight, even after the awful hand holding incident, Kurt moved in to kiss me. Right before it happened, I thought I would throw up if he kissed me. But, I decided I had to give it a shot. He kissed me, and it was the most disgusting thing ever. He is attractive, and he's a great guy, but the thought of his tongue in my mouth was horrible. The feeling was even worse."

Taylor's head leaned slightly to the side as she listened. "Do you like kissing at all?" she asked.

"I love kissing, when it's good, but it's so hard to find anyone I want to kiss—that I can kiss," Jordan said. "Most of the time, I find the thought slightly grotesque. Maybe I'm just screwed up or something, but I don't want to kiss most of the men I date. I don't know what I want."

"Whoever it is you want, that's the type of person you need to be going after," Taylor said. "You don't need to be dating these guys who don't do it for you. When you think about kissing, who do you think about kissing?"

Jordan looked down at the ground, knowing that it was now or never.

Looking back up to meet Taylor's gaze and to look her right in the eye, she felt a surge of confidence.

"You," she said.

Jordan watched as a war waged in Taylor's eyes. She had seen the initial attraction and the smoldering blaze, but she also saw restraint and conflict.

"Please say something," Jordan finally managed, all of her confidence gone.

"You haven't been drinking, have you?" Taylor asked cautiously.

"Of course not," Jordan said. "I haven't had a drop."

"And, you want to kiss me?" Taylor asked, the corner of her mouth turning up into a smile that sent a shiver of excitement through Jordan's body.

"More than I've ever wanted to kiss another person," Jordan said.

Without another word, Taylor moved closer to Jordan on the couch. The simple move—and the knowledge of what was coming—made Jordan's breathing heavier.

Taylor reached up and cupped Jordan's chin in her hands. The intensity as her blue eyes stared at Jordan made it seem as if Taylor could see into her soul. There was no question now that they were smoldering with a hungry desire.

"I'm going to kiss you—if that's what you want," Taylor said gently. "If you want me to stop—or if you change your mind in the next couple of seconds, just say so."

Jordan couldn't take it anymore. She had never felt such intensity. Grabbing the back of Taylor's head, she leaned in for the kiss, crossing the little distance that remained between them. As their lips met, Jordan felt desire course through her body. It deepened as Taylor threw her arms around Jordan's body and pulled her closer, while their tongues seemed to dance. Taylor had the softest lips she had ever felt, and Jordan felt herself weaken under their caress.

With each movement, Taylor was sending waves of arousal through Jordan's body. Too quickly, the kiss ended and Taylor pulled back.

The desire clouding her eyes was evident, as was her unspoken question.

"That…" Jordan's voice trailed off as she fought to catch her breath. "That was incredible."

She felt chills up her arms as she replayed the kiss in her mind. That was what a kiss was supposed to feel like.

Without waiting for approval from Taylor, Jordan leaned in and continued the kiss. Taylor reciprocated and deepened the kiss before pulling back briefly.

"Please don't stop," Jordan pleaded breathlessly.

Taylor smiled, and it almost sent Jordan over the edge. She had never felt such sheer and raw attraction.

Instead of stopping, Taylor slid Jordan down so she was lying on the couch with Taylor hovering over her.

For a fleeting second, Jordan feared where this might go. She had never done this, and her heart was racing. But with one look into Taylor's eyes, she knew that she would be happy with whatever happened.

Taylor leaned down and her lips began to play with Jordan's lips, all the while keeping eye contact. She skimmed her teeth lightly around Jordan's bottom lip and pulled it into her mouth. As she sucked gently on Jordan's lip, Jordan felt her entire body tense with passion.

Feeling as if she couldn't move as a result of the desire she felt, she whimpered slightly in pleasure. Her whimpers were cut short as Taylor once again plunged her tongue into Jordan's waiting mouth.

Jordan reached up and tangled her fingers into Taylor's hair, holding on tight and pulling Taylor closer to her.

She angled her hips to close the distance between her body and Taylor's.

Taylor slowly pulled back.

"We shouldn't do that," she said huskily.

"Shouldn't do what?" Jordan breathed.

"Not tonight, anyway," Taylor said. "I care about you a little too much to rip your clothes off and go at it right now. And, if you pull me in like that, I don't know if I'll be able to control what I'm feeling right now."

Jordan wanted to protest. "I've never wanted anyone like I want you." She was so turned on, she knew it would be painful to stop now.

"I want you too, but I want you to be sure. I don't know if you know what you're doing to me right now."

Jordan tried to lock her legs around Taylor's waist, but Taylor sat back on her knees and offered a hand to Jordan to help her up.

"Here," she said. "Let's take a little bit of a breather."

Knowing Taylor was right, Jordan sat up next to her. Still, knowing it was right did nothing to calm the storm of desire she felt.

"I don't want to stop," she said with a frustrated shrug. "For the first time in my life, I don't want to stop."

Taylor took her hand and brought it to her lips. "Jordan, I don't want to stop either, but I want you to be sure you want to do this, and I want to make sure you're ready."

"What do I need to do to get ready?" Jordan asked innocently.

Taylor's smile grew. "There's no protocol or instruction pamphlet. I just want you to think about it first. I mean, you are a virgin. This is a big deal, and I want to make sure you want to do this. I'm not going to take advantage of how you feel right now, no matter how badly I want to sleep with you."

"You want to sleep with me?" Jordan asked with a devilish grin.

"Was that ever in question?" Taylor shot back with a wink.

The move filled Jordan with renewed desire. Even so, she fought to respect the boundary Taylor had erected.

"Thank you for respecting me enough to make sure that I'm ready," Jordan said. "But, to be honest, I wish you would just put down your guard and fuck me."

It was the first time she had ever spoken those words aloud, and she watched as they started a fire in Taylor's eyes.

Taylor leaned over and gently kissed Jordan's earlobe. Taking it in between her teeth, she bit gently and sucked before moving to whisper in her ear. "You're pretty damn sexy and I promise that one day soon I will make love to you." The heat of her breath made Jordan's heart race. "Then, I'll hold you until you're ready again, and at that point, I will fuck you until you scream."

Jordan trembled at the words, for the first time wanting nothing more than to fall into Taylor and give into the desires of her body.

"For now, though," Taylor continued to whisper as she moved down to kiss Jordan along her collarbone, "I will simply kiss you and give you time to consider your decision."

With that, she took Jordan in her arms once again and kissed her, making Jordan suddenly understand the phrase "weak in the knees."

"If you're not going to give in, I think you should probably stop kissing me," Jordan gasped. "It's the last thing I want, but you're making me crazy."

Taylor leaned back and smiled. "You're making me pretty crazy too," she said. "What if we eat a little ice cream and then I'll leave you to think about your decision?"

Jordan nodded. The only decision she wanted to make was to throw caution to the wind and, for once in her life, live wildly. But she knew that Taylor had a lot of life experience, and if she thought it was a good idea to wait, she had a reason.

Taylor handed Jordan the carton of somewhat melted ice cream and grabbed a spoonful for herself. As if sensing Jordan's internal questioning, Taylor cautioned, "It's just a good idea to make sure you're ready. I care about you too much to allow you to make that big a decision on a whim with me."

Jordan shook her head but Taylor held up her hand in response. "I promise, Jordan, you'll feel better if you take some time to think about it. I don't want to be the one who moves too quickly with you. You are far too special for that."

The words touched a part in Jordan's soul that had seemed dead for so long. Someone this incredible thought she was special. She knew she was in some way special, but having Taylor feel the same sent her heart soaring.

As they finished up their ice cream, Jordan wanted nothing more than to take Taylor back to her bedroom.

"Have a good night," Taylor said, leaning down to plant one single kiss on Jordan's head.

"You too," Jordan said, trying to disguise her disappointment. "Thank you for tonight."

Taylor winked and walked out the door.

Jordan tried to figure out what was going on in her head. For years, she had suppressed everything she had felt for women, but now it was undeniable. She felt tears once again sting the corners of her eyes, and this time she didn't fight them.

Taylor had been right about one thing.

She needed time to figure this whole thing out before she made any big decisions.

CHAPTER SEVEN

As she wrapped up her morning jog, Maggie Weston reveled in how the sun streamed through the sky, creating a canvas of beautiful colors in the early morning light.

At times like this, it seemed like there was nothing in the world that could go wrong. The birds sang sweetly overhead, and each of her muscles ached in a way that showed that her workout was working. She closed her eyes and took a long, deep breath, rejoicing in the calm of the moment.

She knew all too well that it would be over soon, and it would all come crashing back into her like a rogue wave. It had been a rough year. Between regular everyday stressors, her daughter had been at the forefront of her worries for some time now.

As she made her way back to the house, she envisioned how Jordan had been as a young girl. Always so full of life and so much larger than life. Her green eyes always sparkled with a hint of mischief and with a fire that only a dreamer could show. Her goals and dreams had lifted her through so much of her life, and she had always been working toward something. She pushed harder, ran faster, and worked more diligently than anyone Maggie had ever known. That intensity carried over to the way that Jordan loved and cared for those around her.

It had all changed when she got injured. It was now as if Jordan were a lost girl, no longer tethered to any goals or plans. It had taken its toll on Jordan—and on the family as well. It was hard to see Jordan so uncertain and so confused.

Giving in to her stress, without conscious thought Maggie brought her index finger to her mouth and started biting her nail. As soon as she realized what she was doing, she scolded herself.

Like mother, like daughter. They had always been so much alike—even straight down to their bad habits—but now she didn't know how to help.

In the house, her cell phone buzzed on the kitchen counter. It was early, and the call startled her until she remembered that it was the first Monday of the month. It was her monthly morning chat with one of her best friends.

"Good morning," Maggie answered, as she headed back outside to sit on the patio to enjoy some sunshine while she chatted with Janelle.

"Good morning to you, too," Janelle responded. "How are you doing today?"

"I'm honestly having somewhat of a rough day," Maggie said, suddenly letting go of her need to keep the issue quiet.

"What's going on?" Janelle questioned warmly.

She always seemed so sincere, and Maggie felt like she could trust her. Besides, she needed advice on what to do for Jordan. Janelle's kids always seemed happy enough, and maybe another mother could shed some light on the situation.

"It's Jordan," she said. "I don't know how to help her. She's been going through a really tough time in her life, and I feel like she's losing herself."

"She's been coming to the young adults group at the church, hasn't she?" Janelle asked.

"She actually has," Maggie said. "Maybe I'm blowing the whole thing out of proportion, and maybe she'll be back to her old self after a few more weeks of regular church time. I just can't stop thinking that she deserves more happiness from life than she's allowing herself. I'm afraid she's selling herself short and taking this basketball thing much harder than she needs to. I'm probably overreacting. I'm just used to seeing my smiling, sunshiny Jordan. I miss her."

"Well, a mother always knows best when to be concerned," Janelle said. "Maybe she just needs to talk about it all with someone. Will she open up to you?"

Maggie considered the question. As a young girl, there was nothing at all that Jordan kept a secret from her. She was always the first to confide in her mom, and the two had developed an unparalleled closeness compared to any mother and daughter relationship she had encountered. But, this was different. This time, it didn't seem like Jordan wanted to talk to anyone.

Finally she answered, "No, I don't think she will—not about this anyway."

"Well, I happen to know a pretty nice counselor if you think she might open up to someone outside her family," Janelle said with a laugh.

"Do you think she would?" Maggie asked, asking herself the same question. "She's known you for years."

"Yeah, but she hasn't really been around me that much lately," Janelle said. "Besides, I have a confidentiality law. I'm not allowed to tell anyone—including you—anything we talk about in that room."

"Okay," Maggie said, trying to convince herself. She had never imagined she would be the type of person with a daughter in therapy, and she never imagined that her daughter would need therapy. It was all a little too much to deal with this morning, but she knew that Jordan would be in good hands with Janelle.

She took a deep breath to move forward with what she knew she needed to do. "You've always been a good friend to me, Janelle," Maggie said. "I know you'll take good care of my Jordan, and I think maybe we should set up an appointment."

As they hashed out the details of Jordan's class schedule and when they could schedule the appointment, Maggie second-guessed her decision. She remembered the people who had warned her not to trust Janelle at the beginning of their friendship. She recalled the ugly things they had said. According to this backbiting little town, Janelle was a liar, a gossip and couldn't be trusted.

Reminding herself of Janelle's years of loyal friendship, she cast those thoughts aside. For years, she had been a friend, and she cared about Jordan. She would help Jordan.

Forcing positive thoughts, Maggie put down her protective mother claws and booked the appointment.

"Do you think she'll show up?" Janelle asked.

"I hope so," Maggie said. "Too bad she's not little enough anymore to trick by telling her I'll take her for ice cream."

They both laughed.

"Do you know if she has been enjoying the young adult group?" Janelle asked.

"I think she has," Maggie answered. "Every time I've asked her about it, she has said that the group is all right, and the people are pretty cool. Those are her words, at least."

Janelle laughed. "At least our church has cool people, I guess. We've got to keep those young people coming back somehow."

Maggie agreed, and as they wrapped up their conversation, she convinced herself she had done what was best for her daughter. She hoped that soon she would have her daughter back and as full of life as she had always been.

Yet she couldn't help but feel like she had betrayed the trust that she and Jordan had always shared. They hadn't kept secrets from one another, they didn't trick each other and they certainly didn't go behind each other's backs. Yet, that's just what she had done.

With a deep breath, she dismissed her thoughts. Jordan needed help.

* * *

Making the addition to her appointment book, Janelle shook her head. She truly did feel for Maggie. As one of her oldest friends, the last thing she wanted was for Maggie's daughter to go through a tough time or to make poor decisions.

She thought of her own son and all the trouble that he was going through, and she silently vowed that she would not stand idly by and let Jordan go through anything similar.

Although she had not actually seen Jordan in a few years, she remembered her as a vivacious, sweet little thing with such a positive attitude. It pained her to think that the smiling girl who could light up an entire room might be disappearing forever. She would do everything in her power to ensure that was not the case.

For reasons that she couldn't explain, her hands were shaking when she picked up her phone. She was going to have to do a better job of not being so damn insecure.

"Hi, Jordan," Janelle said warmly. "It's Janelle—your mother's friend."

There was a slight pause. "Hi, Janelle," Jordan said, confusion in her voice. "Is something wrong? My mom is okay, isn't she?"

"Everything is fine," Janelle said, feeling guilty for having woken the girl up in a panic. "I actually just got off the phone with your mom a little bit ago. She gave me your number and asked if I would give you a call."

"Okay," Jordan said slowly.

Janelle stifled a laugh. She couldn't imagine what it would be like to be on the other end of this call, having no clue what was happening.

"She told me you've been going to the young adults group at our church," Janelle said, hoping to ease her nerves and guide her into easy conversation.

"I am," Jordan said. "I've actually been enjoying it quite a bit."

"Good. I'm glad to hear that. I really am."

"Thanks," Jordan said awkwardly. "What else did my mom tell you?"

Leave it to a young person to always have suspicions.

"She said you've been going through somewhat of a tough time," Janelle answered cautiously.

"I really don't think that's any of my mom's business to be spreading," Jordan said sternly. "I appreciate the call, but I'm fine."

The sweet, good-natured Jordan whom Janelle had once known was not the girl on the phone today. The thought upset her.

"She didn't go into detail, honey," Janelle said gently. "She just said you might need someone to talk to. I'm a counselor, and she thought maybe I could help."

"I know you're a counselor," Jordan said. It was obvious that she was trying to keep the edge out of her voice, but she was clearly irritated. "I do not need therapy. I am fine."

"It's not therapy, Jordan," she said. "It's just a chance to talk to an old friend about what's going on in your life. It's a chance to open up and shed some of what has been bothering you."

Jordan sighed. "My mom already booked me an appointment, didn't she?"

Her tone was defeated, but that made Janelle happy. It sounded as if she would give in if her mother called the shots.

"She actually has," Janelle said. "But she did so around your class schedule, and it's totally up to you whether or not you show up."

She hated giving her an out, but she knew it was often essential to ensure that clients didn't get cold feet and run. They had to think this was their idea.

"I don't really have a choice," Jordan said. All of the fire had gone out of her voice. "When is it?"

"Tomorrow at noon," Janelle said. "We don't even have to meet at my office. I was thinking maybe we could go to a restaurant and grab some lunch to make it a little more casual."

"Is your office at the church?" Jordan asked.

"It is."

"Okay," Jordan said. "I will meet you there at noon. I was going to swing by there anyway."

"What are you doing at the church tomorrow?" Janelle asked, trying to hide the overt curiosity.

"I am meeting a friend," Jordan said. "Anyway, I'll see you tomorrow. Thanks."

With that, Jordan disconnected the call. Janelle had a pretty good idea which "friend" Jordan was going to see. Taylor occasionally had friends for coffee in the church lounge. Janelle had heard Pastor Reeves explaining one day that it was her way of reaching out and bringing people into the church. The way Janelle saw it, it was simply her way of bringing people in to make them take her side in matters that should be none of her concern. She had a way of forming an army of allies. Even in the short time Taylor had lived here, Janelle had witnessed it.

The thought disgusted her. That was probably why the girl was so depressed. She was spending far too much time associating with bad influences.

* * *

Jordan placed her phone on the kitchen table and immediately burst into tears. Her mom had no clue how fucked up she was, and with the very little she actually knew she still thought that Jordan needed therapy.

Looking down at her shaking hands through blurry tears, she wanted to be anywhere but here. She wanted to be back into her place of denial. And, for a fleeting moment, she wished she had never met Taylor Reeves.

CHAPTER EIGHT

"The mail is here," a voice called from the kitchen.

"I'll go get it," she piped up, eager to get out of the house full of screaming children.

Even at eleven years old, she knew how important a little time alone was to her, and she knew that if she didn't get it, she would get even more annoyed. She was tired of her cousins coming over, and she wanted a little fresh air. Every time they came over, it seemed like they teased her more and more. They were relentless and mean.

She recognized that she was not the typical girl who wanted to play with dolls and play house. Usually, her friends at school were all boys, and they let her join in with their fun games. Her cousins, on the other hand, were all boys and seemed to delight in leaving her out of the fun.

They called her names far too often, and they made her feel ashamed for being a tomboy. Today, even her mother had agreed with them.

"You need to act like a little lady," she had scolded, much to the boys' delight.

They had stood behind her mom, sticking out their tongues and mocking Jordan, making her feel even more alone. She needed to get away from them—all of them—even if only for a few minutes.

Bounding out the door, she relished the beauty of the sunshine on her way to the mailbox. Just for fun, she let her guard down and danced crazily on the sidewalk. For these moments there was no one to tell her that she was not being ladylike or that she needed to stand up straight.

Even though there would be nothing for her in the mail, she went through the stack of paper. At the bottom, she found a department store catalog.

Her smile grew. If she couldn't be one of the boys today, at least she would have something to keep her somewhat entertained while they had all the fun playing cops and robbers or jumping in mud puddles in the backyard.

On the way back to the house, she stooped and buried her hands in the dirt. Setting the mail to the side, she let herself get lost in the beauty of letting go of all that was supposedly "ladylike." She hated that word, even though she wasn't quite sure why. It just seemed to suggest that she had to be something else—as if whatever she already was just wasn't good enough. Her dad didn't ever seem to mind that she liked to play outside or that she was more interested in basketball than learning to cook or clean.

Finally, she stood with a sigh and gathered the mail. She set it on the hall table for her mother—all except for the catalog. Casting a sideways glance at the boys, she decided to not even give them the satisfaction of asking if she could play with them. She took a seat on the couch and began to flip through the pages.

It was nothing too exciting—just this spring's JC Penney catalog. She looked through the pages of dresses and knew her mother would love it if she would ask for one of them. She would probably scrape together the money, just to have her little girl dressed all in pink.

With a disgusted sigh, she flipped the pages. Boy clothes, men's clothes, baby clothes. There was nothing of interest, aside from the few pages of toys—most of which she knew she couldn't ask for anyway. They didn't have the money, and she could just imagine her mother's disgust if she were to ask for a remote control car.

"Don't you want to play with a Barbie doll?" her mother would ask.

Moving past the toys, she searched for anything interesting. She had almost given up and flipped the catalog closed when her eye caught a glimpse of something intriguing on the next page.

As she flipped the page fully open, she felt a slight shiver run through her body. Her eyes widened as she took in the sight of the full-figured beauty on the page.

For the first time, she felt the hormones everyone had been talking about begin to stir. It was as if something inside her had awakened. She tried to stare at the girl's deep brown eyes, but her own eyes gravitated lower, without her permission.

She felt her breathing get heavier as she stared, for the first time understanding attraction.

"Ew!" She heard her cousin's shriek from behind her.

She jumped and slammed the catalog closed. She glared at him over her shoulder.

"You're gross," he said. "Why are you checking out the girls in the bra magazine?"

Her face flushed, she wanted to crawl under the sofa. But she went on the offensive.

"I was looking for me," she said angrily. "Maybe I might need one of those."

"A bra?" The scoffing tone of his voice fueled her anger. "You don't need one. You don't have any boobs. You're flatter than a pancake. You were just enjoying the view. You're a lesbo, aren't you?"

Instantly, she slapped him across the face.

"Don't you ever call me that again," she yelled. "I am not."

She knew what the word meant, and she knew what she had heard about it.

"Sinful. Disgusting. Wrong." Her father would spout off every ugly word he could think of every time anything was mentioned about someone being gay. They were different. They chose to live lives filled with grossness. She had heard it all, and she didn't want to be grouped into that category. Her protests grew louder, as did the teasing. All around her, it felt as if the world was exploding and she was watching. Her mother yelled, her cousin yelled, she yelled. There was no distinction

between them at all. She was accused, and she was guilty. Even as dirty
as she felt, she continued to defend her motives as nothing but pure.

Jordan woke with a start. Her hands were trembling as she
tried to shake off the realness of the dream. She fought off the
wave of fresh tears that threatened to fall.

The dream was a memory—and at once it came crashing
back into her. For years, she had pushed that memory to the
back of her mind, along with the hours after the confrontation
when she had prayed over and over again, asking God to not
allow her to be a lesbian. Recalling how she had locked herself
in the solitude of her bedroom and prayed all day and night
made her stomach hurt. The pain was raw and fresh, reminding
her that she had tendencies to be something that was not simply
frowned upon—but something that was dirty, impure and
completely unacceptable.

She wanted to stand, but she felt dizzy. Had she known all
this time and simply suppressed the thoughts and desires? In
her heart, she knew the truth, but she still refused to give in to
it that easily.

Forcing a deep breath, Jordan decided she would shower
and then find someone to talk to about all of this. There had to
be a way to sort through all of these crazy thoughts.

Taylor passed through her mind, and more than anything,
she wanted to discuss all of this with her. Somehow, that seemed
to be against the rules, though—at least Taylor's rules.

Still, she would be meeting Taylor at the church for coffee
this morning. The thought sent a new set of excited chills
through her body. There was something so unique about the
way Taylor made her feel. It was unlike anything she had ever
experienced. It filled her with anticipation and made her feel as
if she was entering a new chapter in life. More than anything, it
was unnerving.

* * *

Looking down at the coffee stain on her shirt, Taylor shook
her head. The ease with which her mind had been so distracted
lately was really starting to wear on her.

She hated being dirty, so she quickly put her truck in gear and headed back to her house. After changing clothes quickly, she stood in front of the mirror. There was no question that she was a bundle of nerves this morning.

She hadn't seen Jordan since their kiss—or kisses. In the interest of allowing Jordan to make the decisions that were best for her, Taylor had kept her distance.

Her hormones had chided her daily for the decision, but she wanted Jordan to be sure. She knew—all too well—what it was like to jump headfirst into a life-changing path and get caught up in the tides of lust and love. She also knew the heartache and doubts that could come.

After she had first slept with a woman, she had spent weeks crying because she had always been taught it was wrong. She knew now, of course, that it was not wrong at all. Still, it had taken her a long time to come to terms with it, and she desperately did not want to hurt Jordan in the ways that she had been hurt.

As a result, she had decided that alone time with Jordan was off limits until Jordan knew, without a doubt, what she wanted. Aside from a few text messages, there had been little contact over the last few days.

She stared at herself in the mirror. The tiny crows'-feet forming by her eyes, combined with how young and vibrant Jordan was, made her feel old. She fought the urge to break down in tears.

Just for once, couldn't it be easy? It had always been this way, though. The sneaking around and hiding, the lying, the double life because she was a pastor's daughter. Her love life had never had the easy flow that she so envied in many couples. There would never be the opportunity to take someone home and introduce them to her parents, to get engaged, to ride off into the proverbial sunset together.

She had feelings for Jordan. Jordan had feelings for her. It should have been simple. But it seemed like complication was the only steady factor in her life. Complicated emotion had run rampant through most every relationship she had ever experienced.

"Get it together, Reeves," she chided quietly, steeling herself. She took a deep breath and quickly changed clothes.

On her way back to the church, a Joan Jett song came on the radio. She turned it up loud enough that she didn't have to think. Pushing aside all worries about Jordan, she allowed herself to get lost in the music.

As she sang along, she felt some of the tension leave her body. When she pulled up to the parking lot and saw Jordan standing nervously outside of her car all the tension immediately came back.

Although she was roiling with emotion inside, she parked her truck, smiling like an idiot.

Jordan looked up and returned her smile, but her eyes were clouded with doubt and confusion.

Taylor got out of her truck and threw her arms around Jordan. Her nearness was almost enough to completely unnerve Taylor, but instead she stood strong. Jordan needed a friend.

"It's all going to be okay," Taylor said, squeezing her just a little tighter. "I promise you it will."

Jordan looked into Taylor's eyes, and then turned away.

"What's wrong?" Taylor asked.

"It's hard to look at you," Jordan admitted quietly.

"Ouch." The words hit Taylor harder than she would have liked to admit. She looked down at the ground, trying to regain her composure and take this conversation as normal friendship.

"It's not like that," Jordan said, motioning her hands as though she was searching for the right words. "It's just that no matter how hard I try, I can't see you as just a friend anymore, and that terrifies me."

Her confession twisted the knife in Taylor's heart. Without meaning to, she had turned this poor girl's world upside down and caused her far too much turmoil.

"Let's go inside and grab some coffee, while we discuss this—and everything," Taylor said.

She fought the urge to grab Jordan's hand. It would not be appropriate here outside of her father's office, and she had a feeling it would send Jordan on a full-blown emotional roller coaster.

As they walked in silence, Taylor memorized everything about the way Jordan moved. Today, it was as if caution was guiding her every step. There was a hesitancy in the movements of her body and muddled confusion clouding every expression on her face.

For a fleeting moment, she almost wished they had never kissed. Then dismissed the wish. She knew she would be unhappy had they not. Sure, Jordan's friendship was good enough, but who wanted good enough when you could have mind-blowing, amazing and whirlwind passion? That was exactly what their kisses had been. It had been so surreal that Taylor swore she finally understood the cliché of fireworks going off during a kiss.

She shook her head in an effort to physically shake off the thoughts. Out of the corner of her eye, Taylor glanced at Jordan, only to see that her hands were shaking.

"It's okay," Taylor whispered, trying to reassure her and give her a little comfort.

Jordan just shook her head slowly.

"Do you want to talk out here instead?" Taylor asked, noticing the way Jordan's eyes widened at the church door.

"I think that would be best," Jordan said. "I might burn up if I walk through those doors." As she said the words, the slight grin Taylor had come to love danced on the corners of Jordan's mouth.

"How do I walk through with such ease every day, then?" Taylor challenged.

"I don't know," Jordan said with a shrug. "Your dad is a pastor. Maybe you've got some kind of untouchable, holy blood running through your veins or something."

Taylor laughed at the thought. "I assure you, there's nothing special about me."

She had spoken the words lightly, but she saw a fire blaze in Jordan's eyes that caused a catch in her breath.

"Don't you say that," Jordan said. Her words were quiet but intense. "You are more special to me than you could ever imagine."

As the passion burned through Jordan's eyes and bored into Taylor's, Taylor felt her body quiver.

They sat on the tailgate of Taylor's truck, and Taylor turned to look Jordan in the eye. She watched in pain as Jordan's eyes welled up with tears.

"I just don't know what to do," she said.

Taylor swallowed and nodded. "I can understand that. I'm sorry for causing you so much confusion."

Jordan shook her head quickly. "You didn't do this to me," she said. "I have always wondered. I've always been a little too curious about it all, and now I'm just having to deal with what it means."

"What do you think it means?" Taylor asked.

The tears spilled over onto Jordan's cheek as she shook her head more vigorously. "I can't even think about that possibility right now. I don't want to have to deal with it. No one would understand. My family would disown me, I'd lose my friends, and I'm just not okay with that."

"Okay," Taylor said softly, grabbing Jordan's hand for support. "I understand that—probably better than most people you'll meet. We don't have to talk about it right now if you don't want to."

She pulled Jordan into a hug. "Let's talk about something else for a little while," she said tenderly as she moved away. "How are your classes? It's almost finals week, right?"

Jordan nodded. "They're going fine, I guess," she said. "I haven't really had much time to think about them lately. I'll pass them. I'll get an A in each of them, and then I'll move on. I just kind of wish I was taking summer classes this year."

"Why is that?" Taylor asked.

"I need something to take my mind off all of this, or I might just go crazy," Jordan admitted quietly.

"Don't go crazy," Taylor said with a smile. "I'll be here to help you through any of it—however you need me to be here."

She saw desire dance with uncertainty in Jordan's eyes, and she knew they were both in trouble. The look set off something that had lain dormant inside of Taylor for far too long, and she resisted the urge to break Jordan's confusion with a kiss.

As they sat and talked, it was as if things had gone slightly back to normal, aside from the obviously charged energy that existed between the two of them. They discussed work, school and their families.

After a while, Jordan looked up at Taylor. "Thank you," she said softly.

"What for?"

"For everything," Jordan whispered. "But mainly for making me feel better. I've been in a weird place lately, and I wasn't sure anyone could help. You do, though. You help me all the time."

The words made Taylor smile. "You help me, too, Jordan."

Jordan leaned in and gave her a gentle kiss on the cheek. "You're the best friend I've had," she admitted as she pulled away.

"You're mine, too," Taylor said, smiling at the lingering feeling of electricity where Jordan had kissed her.

They sat, embraced, for a few minutes, before Jordan glanced at her watch.

"I've got to go," she said, jumping down to the ground.

Taylor glanced at her watch in response. "Where do you have to go?"

"My mom set me up an appointment with a counselor," Jordan said with a sigh. "I'm not thrilled about it, but she thinks I'm troubled since I had to quit the team. She says I'm depressed and I'm not myself, but she hasn't seen me lately. I've been great since I met you."

Taylor reached up and wiped away the remaining tear on Jordan's cheek. "Well, great, except for this," she said. "Maybe it will be good for you to have someone to talk to about everything."

"That's why I have you," Jordan said with a shrug. "I don't want to open up to just anyone."

"I understand," Taylor said. "I couldn't do the whole therapy thing. I'm a little too private to tell someone I don't know all about my problems."

"Exactly," Jordan said. "I'm not looking forward to it, but I told my mom I would go so she'd get off my back about it all. Maybe if she thinks I'm going to therapy and talking it all out, she'll stop being so pushy."

"I hope so," Taylor said. "It just might help. Who are you going to see?"

"Janelle Wilson," Jordan said, shaking her head. "She's an old friend of my mom's, so I guess at least I'm not going to a complete stranger to talk about all of life's problems."

Taylor attempted to keep her face neutral, but she felt the color quickly drain from it.

"What's wrong?" Jordan asked. "Do you not like her?"

With everything in her being, she wanted to tell Jordan to blow off the appointment, to run as fast as she could in the opposite direction. That woman was nothing but trouble.

"I just think she can be a little difficult sometimes," Taylor managed. "We don't see eye to eye on a lot of things, and I'm not sure she's the best person for you to talk to, Jordan. I don't want to see you get hurt by anything."

Jordan smiled. "Thank you," she said. "I won't get hurt, though. My mom trusts her, and I've been around her quite a few times throughout the years. My family and theirs used to get together for dinners from time to time. I don't know her incredibly well, but she's a nice enough lady. I plan to go in there and chat about basketball—nothing else."

"Nothing else?" Taylor asked, noting the fact that her heart was now beating much faster than it should. If Jordan said anything about her, it would be catastrophic.

"I won't even mention you," Jordan said. "I know that what happened—or didn't happen—isn't something either one of us wants out in the open."

Taylor breathed a slight sigh of relief, but still she couldn't fight the overwhelming feeling of impending doom. Trouble followed wherever Janelle set foot.

"Don't let her hurt you," Taylor warned. "I just don't trust her."

"It will all be okay," Jordan said. "I promise. I just have to do this for my mom. I'll go a couple of times, and then it'll all be over and I don't have to talk to her again if I think it's a bad idea. I don't imagine this will help me at all anyway, but I'm going to make sure it doesn't hurt me or you—or us."

Taylor nodded, but she felt anything but certain.

"Okay," she finally said, getting down from the tailgate. "Well, good luck. Call me later."

After a quick hug, she retreated back to her office. She refused to look back at Jordan, because everything in her heart told her to rescue the poor girl.

You can't save her, she said to herself. She knew it was true, but she could not stop the desire to do just that.

When she returned to her office, her hands were shaking.

"You look like you've seen a ghost, T," her dad said, following her into the tiny room. He sat across from her desk with genuine concern in his eyes.

She shook her head. "I'm fine, Dad. It's nothing."

"It doesn't look like nothing," he said gently.

The simplicity of his typical argument made her smile slightly. He never pried. He simply opened the door wider and wider until she spilled whatever was on her mind.

"I'm just worried about a friend," she said, hoping that he would let her get away with being slightly vague for once.

"Which friend?" he asked.

"I don't think you've met her," Taylor said. "She comes to our Tuesday group, and she's going through a hard time."

He nodded, allowing for a brief silence.

"She'll be fine," Taylor said, filling the silence. "It's just that I worry about her."

"Don't worry," he said. "Just pray. I'll be praying, too."

She nodded. More than anything, she wanted to pray that Jordan would decide not to meet with Janelle, but she fought the urge to tell her father as much. He knew, all too well, exactly how she felt about that woman and her loyal tribe of gossips. They were really more like a small gang than anything else, and she had grown to despise their destructive ways as soon as she had met them.

"Hang in there, kid," he said, acknowledging that she didn't care to dig deeper into the subject. He stood and kissed her on the top of the head. "It will all be okay. It always is."

"It always is, somehow," she agreed, to appease his worries, silently hoping he was right.

She watched from her office in the back as Janelle came in and made herself at home, cringing as Janelle poured herself a cup of coffee.

For the millionth time, she was thankful that she only spent part of her time in this office. She knew that she would have snapped completely if she had to see that woman every morning.

Without saying a word, she rose from her desk chair and quietly shut her door. If Jordan was going to pour her heart out to that gossip, she wasn't going to watch it happen.

She retreated to her desk and threw herself into the website redesign she was working on. Although she was distracted, she knew that she had to have something to keep her mind off what was happening two doors down.

CHAPTER NINE

The couch was too stiff. It wasn't the first thing Jordan noticed, but it was easier to think about than the fact that Janelle's eyes were boring into Jordan's forehead.

For the first time in years, she felt like a small child—a difficult feat given her tall stature. She wanted to bolt from the room and never come back, but she knew she would never live that down—not with her mother and not with Taylor.

She couldn't explain why, but she wanted to prove Taylor wrong on this one. Taylor had a knack for distrusting people, and Jordan assumed it was simply because she had been burned a time or two, but she didn't want Taylor living life in that scared way. She wanted her to open up, to trust and to see the best in people.

But now, as she looked across the room at Janelle, she felt Taylor's inability to trust manifest itself within her own heart. There was nothing out of the ordinary in Janelle's expression; it was simply that she was terrified of what would come out of her own mouth if she gave herself a chance to talk.

Janelle cleared her throat, breaking through the silence, and making Jordan realize that she had been nervously biting her lip.

"How have you been, Jordan?" Janelle finally asked.

Jordan managed a smile, trying not to look as undone as she felt inside. "I've been well, thank you."

The answer was far too composed and formal. She knew it, but she couldn't change the tone in her voice to make it personal, even if she tried. This was a formality. It was something her mother wanted her to do, and it was something Taylor didn't want her to do. The thoughts collided, creating a strange warring of emotions within her body. Suddenly, she couldn't figure out what she really wanted. Did she want to try to talk through her problems with some woman who was a friend of her mother's? Or, did she want to run screaming from this building and never return?

Instead of figuring out her confusion, she forced herself to focus on Janelle. Her mouth was forming words, but Jordan's thoughts had run amuck, making her lose all sense of focus.

"I'm sorry," Jordan said. "What did you ask?"

Janelle smiled softly. "You can relax, Jordan," she said. "It's me. You've known me and my family forever. You can trust me. And you can open up."

If someone has to tell you that they can be trusted, they probably can't. She willed her subconscious to shut off the unwelcome thoughts and instead straightened on the couch. She nodded, still unsure of what to say.

"You've never done anything like this, have you?" Janelle asked.

"No," Jordan answered. "I've always pretty much had my life together."

Janelle leaned in closer. It should have been intimidating, but for some reason, it put Jordan slightly at ease. "Would you say you don't feel like you have your life together right now?"

Jordan weighed the question in her mind. Finally, she shook her head. "I guess not," she admitted shamefully.

"Don't be ashamed," Janelle said. "You don't always have to have it together."

"But, I should," Jordan said.

"Why?" Janelle's question wasn't a challenge; it was merely a curiosity.

"I've just always been that girl," Jordan said, suddenly feeling the need to unleash some of her thoughts. "You know, I've always been a straight-A student, a basketball standout, a good kid. I've always had the life that people desired, but even more than that, I always had the life I wanted. I was surrounded by a group of friends, and I never had to wonder if I was good enough or important enough. I just knew. I had confidence, I had everything I wanted."

"And, you feel like that's all gone now?" Janelle asked after a second.

Jordan nodded, allowing a tear to slip from her eye. She hated herself for crying in front of someone. Aside from Taylor, she'd kept her emotions to herself. She wasn't the type of girl to break down in front of an acquaintance. "I'm sorry," she muttered, wiping the tear from her cheek.

"You don't need to apologize for how you feel," Janelle said.

The words felt like a knife in Jordan's heart. If only she knew what Jordan was really feeling, she wouldn't be so quick to offer that line. Instead, she would probably react the exact same way Jordan's family would.

She let out a sigh. "Okay," she said, attempting to pull herself back together.

"Why don't you tell me what you don't have now that you once had," Janelle urged.

"Everything," Jordan admitted, shocked at her sudden, brutal honesty.

Janelle allowed the silence to build, until Jordan couldn't take it anymore.

"I lost everything that I held dear," Jordan said. "You know, my perfect life went down the drain right along with my busted knee."

Jordan looked down at her knee again with disdain. For months, she had continually wanted to scream at her own body, *"How could you do this to me?"*

She pushed the thought aside and continued to try to describe how she felt. "My friends disappeared pretty quickly. I mean, they all had other things to do. Most of them are still on the basketball team, and I know how much that sucks up your time. I get it. I really do, but that doesn't mean it didn't hurt when they stopped calling, stopped inviting me to hang out with the group, and just went their own ways."

For the first time, she found herself putting her loneliness into words, and it felt good. Even though she knew she shouldn't spill it all out, she couldn't stop herself.

"It was like basketball was the only thing that connected me to them, I guess," she continued. "All this time, I thought we were lifelong friends. I thought they would be there for me, no matter what. I thought I had a roommate who loved my friendship and a team of girls who cared about me as a person—not just as a ball player. But, the minute it was over, we suddenly had nothing in common. All the laughs we shared, the secrets we kept, and the fun we had just vanished. The few times I did see them, it was like we were different people, suddenly lacking what we had shared. It vanished, and for a while my happiness did, too."

"Did it come back?" Janelle asked after a pause.

Jordan had promised Taylor she wouldn't even mention her name, so instead she simply shrugged. "I guess so," she said cautiously. "I'm just learning to be okay and accept things, I think. That life isn't coming back, and those friends are not going to return like they once were. I'm just focusing on trying to move forward."

"That's good," Janelle said. "How are you moving forward?"

"I'm figuring it out one day at a time," she said, deciding that was the only truthful thing she could say without breaching her agreement with Taylor.

"Okay," Janelle coaxed. "That's good to hear."

There was a slight pause. "How do you like the young adults group at the church?" Janelle asked.

Jordan moved her head from side to side, trying to best determine how to answer the question.

"It's all right," she finally said. "I'm not crazy about the whole group thing most of the time, but there are some pretty cool people there. I like going, because it gives me the chance to hang out with a group of people like I used to, I guess."

"That's good," Janelle said. "Have you met Callie yet? She's the group's leader."

Jordan fought to keep her face from showing any sign of disapproval. Taylor had already voiced her distrust for Callie as well, and Jordan trusted her opinion enough to keep a safe distance.

"I've spoken to her and been introduced during group time," she said. "Beyond that, I don't really know her very well."

"I think the two of you would get along very well," Janelle said. She pulled out a piece of paper and began scrawling on it. "Here," she said, handing the paper to Jordan. "This is her number. I think you should call her and hang out with her a bit. She would be a good influence for you."

There was a bit of hidden meaning in the statement, Jordan could tell. She just wasn't quite sure where it came from or what it meant.

"Thanks," Jordan said, accepting the paper. "I should just go ahead and tell you that I'm probably not going to call her. The idea of cold calling someone to hang out seems a bit creepy to me."

Janelle laughed slightly. "Well, then, maybe you two can talk at this week's group meeting. I'll tell her to come chat with you."

Jordan shook her head. "That's really not necessary. I'm fine. I don't want to be that loner girl that has someone else setting up friend dates for me. Thank you, but I'm fine."

"I insist," Janelle said, holding up her hand to stop Jordan's refusal.

The move angered Jordan slightly. This was therapy, after all. She wasn't supposed to be shushed. She thought about walking out, but forced herself to cool her temper. Her dad was always telling her that her little Irish temper would only get her in trouble if she didn't keep it in check.

Silently, she thanked her father for the words of wisdom and sighed. "Okay, that's fine," she said, relenting.

"Do you hang out with anyone else from the group?" Janelle asked.

She didn't want to lie, so she shrugged. "I've met some pretty cool people there."

"Anyone in particular?"

For the first time during their session, Jordan felt like Janelle was prying too much. She wrinkled her forehead and tried to shake off the feeling. Janelle was a counselor. She was supposed to ask questions. It was her job.

"Not really," she lied, suddenly deciding that was the easier route.

"I thought you and Taylor Reeves had struck up somewhat of a friendship," Janelle commented. "This is the biggest small town in America, you know? Word gets around."

Jordan had always been good at reading people, and she could tell Janelle had to force the passive face that she was putting on. Maybe there really was some tension between the two women.

"Yeah," Jordan said, trying to play it off. "She's pretty cool, I guess."

Janelle looked troubled at Jordan's confession.

"Why did you feel the need to lie about your friendship with her?"

"I didn't," Jordan said, a little too defensively. "I just didn't think to mention it."

"Well," Janelle made the word linger longer than it should have. She leaned closer to Jordan. "As a friend of your mother's, I'll warn you to exercise caution in that friendship."

Jordan felt her cheeks blush red, and chided herself for it.

"What do you mean?" she finally managed.

She hoped her face didn't give away the shame that she felt at Janelle's use of the word caution. She had been anything but cautious since she met Taylor, and now things were even more reckless than ever.

"I only say this because I know you," Janelle said. "What is said in this room stays in this room."

"Okay," Jordan said, in agreement. She hoped that was the case. The last thing she wanted was for all of this to end back up at her mother—or worse, someone like Callie.

"I think she's trouble," Janelle blurted. "I don't think that you need that kind of influence in your life."

"She isn't trouble," Jordan said in Taylor's defense. "I actually find it kind of unfair that you are saying these things about her when she's not even here to defend herself."

"I'm not saying these things about her to everyone," Janelle said. "I'm saying this to you, as a friend. I'm saying that I think you should just be careful about how close you get to her."

"How so?" Jordan challenged. She hated the edge that her voice took, but at this moment her passions had won over. Her temper had been unleashed, and if someone was going to tell her to stay away from the one person she couldn't be without, she wanted to know why.

Janelle sighed. "She is wild," she said. "We've all heard the stories of the way she's lived, and none of us want that for you or for any of the rest of the young adults. We don't need that kind of influence."

Jordan shook her head. "She is a kind-hearted woman, with a love for life. She is strong and compassionate. She is adventurous and has had many wonderful life experiences. She's full of wisdom if you would take the time to get to know her instead of sitting here judging her."

She felt the fury rise inside of her. "In fact, that's why I don't like this therapy thing, or even this whole church thing. You all just sit here and judge people. I hate it."

She tried to stop her words, but they kept spilling out. "If more people were like Taylor, maybe people would like this place."

Janelle's eyes were unreadable, but she was gripping the edge of the desk a little too tightly. Jordan saw how white her knuckles were.

Jordan shook her head. "I think we're done here for today," she said. "I apologize for raising my voice, and I will see you next week."

Without waiting for Janelle to respond, she stood from the couch and walked out of the door.

She popped her head into Taylor's office. "Can I speak with you for a moment outside?" she asked.

Taylor's eyes widened as if she had been caught doing something wrong. Quickly, she composed herself and stood.

"Of course," she said, following Jordan out the door.

Jordan walked quickly and furiously out to Taylor's truck and waited for Taylor to catch up.

"What's wrong?" Taylor called after her.

"I can't stand that hypocritical bitch," Jordan fumed quietly. The words seethed out of her like acid as her entire body shook.

"What did she do to you?" Taylor asked, anger rising in her own voice.

Jordan shook her head. "It wasn't me. She didn't do anything to me."

"Then, what's wrong?"

Jordan knew she shouldn't talk about it, but all she wanted to do was punch Janelle in the face for the way she had spoken about Taylor. That fact alone told Jordan a little too much about how she felt about Taylor, but she ignored that thought.

This was her friend, standing in front of her. This was the person to whom her loyalties were owed.

"She said I shouldn't be friends with you," Jordan said quietly, but with anger still running through every word.

Taylor laughed. "Yeah, she's not a big fan of mine," she said coolly. "Don't let that upset you."

"She doesn't even know you," Jordan said. "I just gave her a piece of my mind in defending you, and you don't even care that she thinks you're bad news."

"If I cared about everyone who thought I was bad news, as you put it, I would spend so many sleepless nights I'd never get to sleep," Taylor said with a shrug. "It really doesn't matter to me what she thinks. She's a hypocritical bitch, just like you said. Her opinion does not mean anything to me."

Taylor pulled Jordan into a hug in an obvious attempt to settle her temper. "Your opinion matters to me, though." She spoke the words gently. "Thank you for defending my honor in there."

Jordan pulled back to stare into Taylor's eyes. "Always," she whispered the word as a promise.

Taylor smiled and ended the embrace before it got too heated in the parking lot of the church.

"So, does this mean you're not going back to therapy?" she asked with a smile.

"No," Jordan said. "I told her I'd be back next week."

"Is that the best idea?" Taylor asked.

Jordan shook her head. "Probably not, but I've got to go back in there and make amends when all I want to do is to reach across the table and show her the error of her ways."

Taylor laughed. "I like this little fiery streak you have going here."

A slow smile spread across Jordan's face. "I'm glad you like it," she said. Suddenly, she felt her playful nature coming to life, and she wanted to flirt. It was a foreign feeling, but she liked it.

She nudged Taylor's arm. "Want to come over later? I'll show you a little more of this fiery side." For good measure, she added a wink and watched as unadulterated lust filled Taylor's eyes.

As Taylor struggled to keep her breathing even, she stiffened visibly. "That sounds like fun," she said slowly. "I thought we'd agreed to keep our distance for a little while, though."

"You can keep your distance if you want," Jordan said casually. "Just know that I'm ready and waiting. So, you can come over later, or you can decide not to. It's your call."

With that, she decided that she'd said enough. She gave Taylor a long hug, making sure to press her breasts against her friend's. It sent a shiver of excitement through her entire body and affected her in places that had only been awakened days before.

"I'll think about it," Taylor said, although the longing in her voice made it perfectly clear that she would, in fact, be coming over later.

Jordan gave her a smile and got into her car. As she drove away, she cast one look back into the rearview mirror. Seeing Taylor standing there, clearly undone, made her tremble. She didn't know much, but she knew she was in deep trouble over her feelings for this woman.

CHAPTER TEN

Looking over the notes from their session, Janelle felt her anger rise. She wanted nothing more than to march into Taylor's office and tell her to leave that girl alone.

There was no doubt from Jordan's quick and decisive defense that Taylor was more than just a casual acquaintance. Yet, Jordan had felt the need to hide it from her in their initial conversation. She couldn't decide if that signaled something dangerous, or if it was merely at Taylor's request that Jordan keep their friendship a secret. Either way, she didn't like it, and she was determined to figure out what was happening. Once she did, she'd use whatever leverage she had to get Taylor out of the church office. It was one thing for her to masquerade around here on Sundays, acting like the perfect pastor's daughter, but it was another thing altogether for her to act like it was her job to help run the church, to be behind the scenes of all the day-to-day operations, and to have a trusted place amongst the young adults group.

Whatever it took, she would bring Taylor down. For now, though, she'd have to lay low.

She had sat in deliberation for far too long, and it was time to take action. Casually, she strolled into the pastor's office.

"How did it go?" he asked, looking up over the top of his reading glasses.

Janelle smiled. She made a point of not indulging the pastor in gossip, although it took every ounce of control she had not to do so.

"It went well," she said. "Very well. Is Taylor still in?"

His brow furrowed in confusion, and she knew she should have played it a little cooler. She never asked to speak to Taylor, and she was aware that he probably knew about their difference in personalities.

"I think she went out for a bit, but she should be back in shortly," he said, craning his neck to look into her empty office.

She supposed she could have done the same without creating an atmosphere of curiosity.

"I'll catch up with her soon," she said before turning to leave.

As she turned, she almost bumped into Taylor as she reentered the office.

"Sorry," Taylor said. "Excuse me."

Janelle attempted unsuccessfully to keep the icy edge out of her voice. "It's fine."

"Looks like she's back," the pastor said, nodding in Taylor's direction with an amused smile.

"Thanks," Janelle said, forcing a laugh and hating the way that he always thought he was funnier than he was in reality.

Taylor walked past her, oblivious to the fact that Janelle had been waiting to talk to her. She followed Taylor to her office and stopped in the doorway, suddenly wishing this interaction could take place somewhere more private, without the watching eye of the pastor.

"Do you have a minute?" she asked, knocking lightly on the doorframe.

Although she was fairly certain she saw a look of disgust in Taylor's eyes, Taylor smiled politely and nodded. Janelle was not going to give her time to change her mind. Instead, she stepped inside and pulled the door closer behind her.

"What can you tell me about Jordan Weston?" she asked, deciding that the direct approach would probably be best.

"She attends our Tuesday night group," Taylor said. "She seems like a nice girl."

Janelle leaned in closer out of curiosity. "And the two of you are friends, right?"

Taylor shrugged. "Yeah, we have spent a little time together. Why?"

There was nothing to suggest that Taylor was uncomfortable or even that she found Janelle's probing alarming, so Janelle continued.

"I just wondered," she said. "I am a little worried about her. I'm a friend of her mom's, and she asked me to make sure that Jordan was doing okay lately."

"She seems fine to me," Taylor said with a smile.

"Well, when are you seeing her again?" Janelle questioned.

A spark of suspicion flashed in Taylor's eyes. "I'm not quite sure," she said. "I bet she will be at the group Tuesday."

Janelle was hoping to get something deeper, something to explain the connection that Jordan obviously felt with Taylor, but this was fruitless.

"What do you two do when you are together?" Janelle asked. "Is Jordan a partier? Has she been acting out?"

Taylor laughed. "She's a good kid," she said. "Trust me, she's doing fine. I don't know why you're asking all these questions."

"I'm just making sure she's doing all right," Janelle tried to reassure her. "I just wouldn't want to see her fall in with the wrong crowd."

"Is the church the wrong crowd?" Taylor inquired.

Janelle's face flushed. She had been caught in her insinuation. "Not at all," she said, rising with her words. "I just wanted to make sure. You know, she is young and impressionable and needs a good example. That responsibility follows whoever is older and wiser and placed in her path to help her out."

"I'll make sure and take good care of her then," Taylor said with a smile still plastered on her face. "I'll make sure she stays away from the rest of the bad eggs at church, as well. Would that help?"

The tension in the air was palpable, as Janelle looked directly into Taylor's eyes. Taylor's smile was unfaltering, as if a challenge hung in the balance between them.

Janelle fought the urge to lash out in anger and instead nodded and exited Taylor's office without another word.

She made her way back to her office and grabbed her cell phone. She quickly opened up her messaging screen and sent Callie all of Jordan's contact information with a note to get in touch with the girl.

As she sat down at her desk, she felt her frustrations grow. All she wanted to do was help that poor girl and keep her away from the train wreck that was Taylor Reeves.

* * *

Stepping out of the office, Taylor put on her sunglasses. The summer sun shone brightly as she made her way to her truck. Once inside, she let out the breath that she hadn't realized she was holding.

There was too much pressure. She felt like she was trying to hold it together for everyone right now. Jordan was testing her. No doubt about that. It had taken every ounce of willpower to stay away from her, and now that she had endured the day—and inquisition—from hell, she was ready to blow off some steam.

Knowing that wasn't how she wanted her first encounter with Jordan to take place, she opted for a quick trip to a convenience store instead.

A Red Bull and a cigarette later, she decided that maybe a stop at Jordan's for dinner would be a good call. She picked up her phone to call, but decided against it. A little surprise never hurt anyone.

Humming happily along with the radio, she let the frustrations of the day slip away from her. She would go have dinner with her new best friend, and all would be well. Janelle's curiosity and her inquiries would be a thing of the past.

Jordan had held her own in her counseling session today, and she could do the same next week. Somehow, Taylor had escaped anyone finding out private details of her life thus far, and she was not about to let this tiny Kansas town change that. Janelle could pry all she wanted, and Taylor was not going to give in. She knew Jordan wouldn't either, so they might as well just enjoy themselves.

When she pulled up in front of Jordan's house, her nerves kicked into high gear. She wasn't quite sure why Jordan made her this nervous. Normally, she was calm and collected. In every relationship she had ever been in previously, she had been the levelheaded one. Dating did not make her nervous, but Jordan severely unnerved her.

Walking to the door, she tried to steady her breath. She needed to get it together. She knocked lightly. In the seconds it took for Jordan to answer the door, she regretted not taking an extra look in the mirror. She wanted to look perfect.

Jordan peeked out the door. "Hey," she said in surprise.

"Hey yourself," Taylor said with a smile. "Mind if I stop by for a few?"

Jordan laughed and opened the door all the way. "Be my guest."

The playful smile that danced on Jordan's lips caught Taylor's breath for a second. "I hope I'm not interrupting anything," she said, even though Jordan was dressed comfily in a pair of white basketball shorts and a T-shirt from her old basketball team.

"Just my dinner party," Jordan said, pointing to the kitchen.

Taylor looked around to where Jordan was pointing to see all the ingredients laid out on the counter to make tacos. "Are you having someone over for dinner?" she asked, suddenly regretting her decision to make it a surprise visit.

"Just my best friend," Jordan said, pulling Taylor into the kitchen. "I was just going to have dinner by myself, which explains my fancy attire."

Jordan pretended to model the basketball shorts and T-shirt she was wearing, and Taylor felt her smile grow. This girl put any Victoria's Secret model to shame in whatever she wore.

"Damn," Taylor said. "I didn't know there was a dress code."

They laughed as Jordan moved around the kitchen, grabbing the necessary items to prepare the food. "If you want to help me slice the vegetables, we can make this go twice as fast," Jordan said.

"I'm happy to help," Taylor said, taking the knife and cutting board from Jordan. As their hands brushed, Taylor felt the sensation all over her body.

Jordan looked into Taylor's eyes, sensing the tension she felt. The intensity of her stare made it clear exactly what Jordan wanted. Instead of taking the moment further, though, Jordan bit her bottom lip and turned away. Watching her bite her lip sent a shiver through Taylor's entire body and made her catch her breath. Jordan's ability to quickly go from confident, sassy and sexy to unsure and cautious was sending her on a roller coaster and making her hormones rage like a teenager. Closing her eyes for just a second to will the thoughts away, she regained her composure.

"It's not a dinner party without some good music," Jordan said as she clicked into the iTunes account on her laptop computer, which sat open on the counter.

"What are we listening to tonight?" Taylor asked as she chopped onion. She loved how easily they had fallen into a comfortable friendship. It just felt natural to be here, in Jordan's kitchen, making dinner as they casually chatted about music. It felt almost as natural as Taylor imagined it would feel to take Jordan into her arms and fuck her senseless. She shook her head to clear the image from her mind and looked up to find Jordan watching her carefully.

"What?" Taylor asked, hoping that her thoughts hadn't been transcribed on her forehead as she feared they probably had been.

Jordan wordlessly shook her head and smiled coyly. "Nothing," she said finally. "What were you thinking about?"

"Nothing," Taylor said too quickly.

"Mmmhmm," Jordan said. "Well, whatever it was, it made you sigh."

Taylor felt herself blush slightly, a new sensation for her. Yet, she decided to stick to her story. "It was nothing," she said. "Did you decide on music?"

"I asked you what you wanted to listen to," Jordan said. "But, when you didn't answer, I made up my mind on my own."

"Okay. What will it be?"

"Wait for it," Jordan said with a wink.

Gone was the girl who had acted somewhat shy at first. Jordan was now in full-blown vixen mode, and it was driving Taylor crazy. Her heart raced as she watched the scene in front of her unfold. It was better than any lap dance or striptease she had ever seen. Just sitting there with a half smirk, her dimple showing, and her eyes dancing with lust, Jordan was undoing every nerve in Taylor's body.

Jordan clicked the play button before dancing across the kitchen to stir the meat. Taylor watched in awe as she added seasonings and smiled over her shoulder.

The music started to play, and immediately Taylor let out a small giggle.

"Anything wrong?" Jordan asked.

"Nice song choice," Taylor said, listening as the beginning of "Taste" by Josh Abbott Band started to play.

Jordan turned to face Taylor, her smile growing. "You know it?" she asked, obviously amused.

Taylor nodded. "I like my share of obscure country bands," she said. "It's part of this fitting in thing here in Kansas. Besides, my friend Amy loves Texas country. Last year, we'd drink and listen to this all the time, amazed that country music could be so sexy—so dirty."

"I thought it got the point across," Jordan said, biting her lip once more as she turned back to the frying pan.

The singer started to croon about kissing various parts of the body, and Taylor felt her knees weaken slightly at the sight of Jordan dancing seductively along with the music.

Unable to resist the temptation any longer, Taylor moved to stand directly behind Jordan. She reached around Jordan's waist and moved Jordan away from the stove, turning off the burner.

She kissed Jordan's neck softly and gently. Caressing the tender area with her tongue, she heard Jordan moan and felt her shiver in her arms.

"Is that what you wanted?" Taylor asked breathlessly.

"That," Jordan said huskily. "And so much more."

Needing no further invitation, Taylor spun her around and pushed her up against a section of the counter and let herself get lost in the complete pleasure of lust.

Their lips intertwined and their tongues danced as both of them let out small moans of pleasure.

Jordan pulled back slightly, and Taylor worried she had done something wrong. "Are you okay?" she asked.

"Fuck," Jordan said breathlessly. "I'm more than okay. I'm pretty damn good."

"Why did you stop, then?" Taylor asked.

Jordan smiled. "I just wanted to let you know how much I love it when you kiss me like you want to fuck me."

The words sent Taylor over the edge, and she pressed her body up closer to Jordan's so that Jordan could feel every movement she made as she moved her hips slowly in a grinding motion.

As she deepened the kiss, she felt Jordan's body shake. They both felt the passion, and Taylor knew she couldn't fight it if she tried.

Jordan wrapped her arms around Taylor's head, and as Taylor moved back down to kiss her neck one more time, she felt Jordan practically melt into her arms. Jordan tangled her fingers in Taylor's hair and pulled her in closer as Taylor nibbled on her earlobes. Taking her time, Taylor returned to kiss Jordan's lips before removing her shirt. Silently, she gazed into Jordan's eyes to ask for permission.

Nodding her head vehemently, Jordan in response ripped off Taylor's shirt. There was a hunger in her eyes that Taylor needed no help to understand.

As they tore at each other's clothes, Taylor lifted Jordan up and sat her on the counter.

"Tell me what you want," Taylor coaxed, needing to hear the words come directly from Jordan.

"I already told you," Jordan said, her voice darkened by lust. "I want you to fuck me."

The low moan of passion that slid out of Taylor's throat as she kissed Jordan again surprised even her. She moved Jordan off the counter and took her by the hand.

"Not here," she said. "Someday, maybe, but I want your first time to be special."

Jordan smiled as she moved ahead of Taylor and practically dragged her into the bedroom.

"Will this work?" Jordan asked seductively.

Taylor was unable to speak at the sight of Jordan standing before her in nothing but a bra and basketball shorts. She simply nodded. Taking Jordan in her arms once more, she pulled off the last remaining articles of clothing before taking a step back to revel in the sight before her.

There was no doubt Jordan was the most beautiful girl she had ever seen. Her eyes widened as she took it all in. From her perfect, rounded breasts to her long, lean legs, every part of her looked attractive. Taylor let out a sigh of contentment mixed with sheer desire and ran her fingers over Jordan's flat stomach and up across her toned arms, before wrapping her arms around her and moving her onto the bed.

She laid Jordan on her back and moved to straddle her. Leaning down, she took one of Jordan's hardened nipples into her mouth and caressed it with her tongue, causing Jordan to cry out. She continued to suck, while running her hands up and down Jordan's body.

"I can't take it anymore," Jordan said, much later, through pants. "I need you to fuck me now. I'm wet. Wetter than I've ever been."

Taylor smiled at the words and pulled back to look deep into Jordan's eyes, before sliding her hand down in between Jordan's thighs. Gently circling, she found that Jordan had given an accurate description of how turned on she was. Slowly, she slid one finger inside, easing Jordan into the experience, before sliding down on the bed to taste her. Jordan moaned at the contact, arching her hips and throwing her head back against the pillows.

Taking cues from her body language, Taylor continued slowly, tenderly, until Jordan let out a scream, and her entire body tightened. Taylor looked up to take in the sight of surprised pleasure as Jordan's eyes rolled back into her head and she collapsed back on the bed.

Moving back up to lay beside her, Taylor caressed Jordan's hair and gave her a long, slow kiss. "Was it okay?" she asked, even though she was pretty sure she knew the answer.

"Fuck okay," Jordan said breathlessly. "It was mind-blowing. Thank you."

"Anytime," Taylor replied, kissing her on the forehead.

"Give me just a minute to recover, and then you can walk me through what I need to do to make you feel that good," Jordan said, leaning her head against Taylor's chest.

"Tomorrow," Taylor said. "Tonight was about you, and trust me, I enjoyed that more than just about anything in the world."

Jordan looked for a moment like she might protest, but Taylor shook her head and pulled Jordan closer against her into a spooning position. Holding onto her, she knew she was in trouble. She could stay like this all night and be happy.

In her mind, she replayed the words to one of her favorite poems by Mario Benedetti.

O sea
Resumiendo
Estoy jodido
Y radiante
Quizá más lo primero
Que lo Segundo
Y tambien
Viceversa.

It was some of the only Spanish she knew, but the translation had always stuck with her, and in the silence of the moment, it summed up exactly how she felt. *I'm fucked, and radiant. Perhaps more the former than the latter and vice versa.*

Getting lost in Jordan Weston was a beautiful disaster.

* * *

As she lay still shaking in Taylor's arms, Jordan was positive there was nowhere else she wanted to be. Ever.

Taylor gently kissed her back, and Jordan felt the sensation spread through her still sensitive body. She shivered from the touch and turned to face Taylor.

For a moment, she simply stared into Taylor's eyes, simply reveling in the knowledge that she had never felt such an intensity of pleasure.

"How do you feel?" Taylor asked, her words sliding across the distance like honey.

"I don't even know how to put it into words," Jordan said with a shy grin. "Incredible. Insane. Insatiable."

Taylor's smile grew. "Good," she said. "Me too."

Caught up in the comfort and bliss of the moment, Jordan rested her head on Taylor's chest and then reached for her again.

CHAPTER ELEVEN

Maggie's tank top clung to her body from the morning's spin class, and she rolled down the car windows. The summer air flowed across her skin, bringing a calming sensation. It was a foreign feeling these days. Most of the time, her thoughts centered on Jordan and how she could be helped. There was no question in her mind that her daughter was flailing, looking for something solid to hold onto. The problem was that she had no idea how to help.

As she pulled her car into the driveway, she sat and looked at the house for a moment.

It had been Jordan's childhood home, and she recalled sweetly how her bubbly little girl used to bound from the front door, clad in basketball shorts and a tank top with a basketball in hand. If only she could find someone who made her as happy as that silly sport had always made her, her dear daughter would be back on her feet.

She sighed, knowing that if she broached the subject with Jordan, it would only serve to make her daughter unhappier. She could hear Jordan's voice in her head: "Mom, stop pressuring me!"

It wasn't about pressure. It was merely her desire to see Jordan happy and fulfilled.

She pulled out her cell phone and dialed Jordan's number but hung up before leaving a voice mail. She tried to stave off her tendency to jump to the worst possible conclusion at the drop of a hat, to infringe on Jordan's privacy. Still, it was her duty as a mother to be worried and to want the best for her child. She rationalized what she knew was an overstep of her boundaries and again picked up the phone.

"Good morning," Janelle answered in a chipper voice.

"Hi, Janelle," Maggie said. "How are you doing?"

The two exchanged pleasantries and caught up on life briefly, before Maggie cut to the chase.

"How is she?"

Janelle didn't need any more of an explanation, and the tone in her voice conveyed the type of sympathy only another mother could give.

"I think she's going to be okay," Janelle said slowly. "She's in a rough patch right now, and I'm going to hopefully keep seeing her. We have another meeting scheduled next week. I am slightly worried about the company she's keeping these days, though."

Maggie's curiosity was piqued. "Is it just a wrong crowd situation?"

"I'm not sure." Janelle's voice was hesitant. "You know I'm not supposed to disclose this kind of information. But, as a friend, I would just advise you to talk to her. Ask her who she's hanging out with and try to steer her in the right direction."

"Who should I be worried about?"

"Taylor Reeves." The name rolled out of Janelle's mouth, like a fire engulfing a dry valley. "I shouldn't have said that," Janelle said quickly. "But, just know that I think they're spending a lot of time together, and I'm not sure it's entirely a healthy situation for Jordan."

"What's wrong with the pastor's daughter?"

"Nothing. Look, I've got to go, but I'll call you after our next session."

Janelle quickly said her goodbyes, leaving Maggie more perplexed than ever. If you couldn't trust your daughter to the friendship of the pastor's kid, who could you trust?

In her mind, she recalled all of the kids she had known growing up who were children of pastors, and her questions were put to rest. They were the ones who spent most of their time partying and breaking the rules. They were the wild ones, and even more dangerously, they were the ones who had learned early on in life how not to get caught. They were masters of hiding things, talking their way out of trouble, and generally skating by without reprimand. Janelle was probably right. There was no need for Jordan to get wrapped up in that kind of behavior, even though when she met Taylor, she seemed like a perfectly nice kid.

Once more, she tried to call Jordan. If nothing else she wanted to hear her voice, to know she was okay. If she was getting into some kind of wrong behavior, Maggie wanted to know.

There was still no answer.

"What's wrong?" her husband asked as soon as she entered the house.

"I just have a lot on my mind."

She didn't want to get into it. She already knew what he would say, and it wasn't the answer she was looking for. Brushing past him, she grabbed a glass and filled it with ice water, all the while knowing he was watching her every move intently.

"Care to share?" he prodded.

After taking a long sip, she shook her head. "Not really."

"Are you doing that stressed out Mommy thing again?"

"How did you know?"

"It's been almost thirty years," he said with that same little smirk that had captured her heart so many years ago. "I can tell when you're upset, and more specifically, I can tell when you have the look of a mother bear trying to protect her cub. What's going on?"

"I'm not sure," Maggie admitted, taking a seat at the kitchen table. "I just worry about her."

"It's been an adjustment for her—for all of us, actually. But she's going to get through it."

His words did little to soothe the aching place in her heart, the place that wanted nothing but the best for her little girl. "I'm going to go see her today," Maggie said, making up her mind to do something about it instead of just worrying away the day.

"Does she know you're coming?" Paul asked, furrowing his brow slightly. "She is a grown woman, you know, and she'd probably appreciate a heads up."

"Who made you the boss?" she asked him playfully, trying to get past her nagging worry. "I'll give her another call when I'm on my way over. I think we could both benefit from a day together."

Paul's expression was amused, but there was no doubt that he thought it was a bad idea. She wanted to get angry but knew that an argument would only prolong the morning at home and make her more upset.

He hadn't always been the picture of the parent who respected space. She remembered all too well the nights he had spent analyzing Jordan's every move to make sure that nothing she did jeopardized her athletic career in any way.

With her mind made up, she quickly showered and got ready. She was going to go see her daughter and at least let her know that she could talk to her mother if she needed anything.

* * *

Taylor opened her eyes to morning sunlight streaming in through the blinds. A feeling of pure bliss washed over her entire being as she looked down at Jordan sleeping in her arms.

There was no doubt in her mind that this girl had gotten to her in a way that no one ever had, and she could only hope that

Jordan felt the same way. She watched as Jordan dreamed and wondered what she was dreaming. Tenderly, she brushed a dark hair back from her face and leaned down to kiss her naked back. Covering her in gentle, soft kisses, she let herself get lost in all that Jordan was and all that they could be together.

When Jordan started to stir, she stopped and propped herself up on the pillows.

Slowly, Jordan rolled over to face her. "That felt incredible," she said in a husky voice.

"What did?"

"Your kisses on my back."

Taylor smiled. "I couldn't help it," she admitted. "I just enjoy kissing you."

"I enjoy it, too."

Her words were reassuring, but the look on Jordan's face gave evidence of her uncertainty. "Are you okay?" Taylor asked, stroking her face.

Jordan swallowed and closed her eyes for a minute before nodding. "I'm good," she said with a smile that didn't quite reach her eyes.

Taylor recognized the look all too well. It was the same one she had worn when she was wrestling with her own sexuality. Her desire for Jordan's affection was outweighed by how much she cared about her friend, as she offered the words that cut her to her core. "We don't have to do that again if you don't want to. We can just go back to being friends if that's what you need."

"I think I just need some time to figure it all out," Jordan said with a sigh. "It's not that I didn't enjoy it, or that I don't want to do it again. It's just that I'm scared."

The beeping of Jordan's phone cut off her sentence.

Jordan looked thankful for the distraction and jumped out of bed immediately, scurrying over to the dresser to pick up her phone.

"Shit!"

"What's wrong?" Taylor asked, gazing at her with a million conflicting thoughts running through her mind.

"My mom's tried to call me several times." She picked up the phone. Her eyes widened as she listened to the voice mail.

"Is everything okay?" Taylor asked.

"You have to go right now," Jordan said in a panicked voice. "My mom is on her way over."

Taylor got out of bed and started putting on her clothes.

"We'll talk later," Jordan said hurriedly, all but pushing Taylor out her front door.

Wanting to protest, detesting being treated like a criminal, she tried to understand the situation Jordan was in. With a sigh, she started her truck and pulled out of the parking lot just as a silver car pulled in.

She drove until she was out of town a few miles and pulled over near a field. She got out of the truck and popped her tailgate down to take a seat, suddenly thankful for rural Kansas and its peacefulness. It seemed to make the decision-making process a little easier—or at least a little less distracting.

Leaning her head back to take in the way the sun glimmered off the wheat, she tried to put herself in Jordan's shoes. The girl definitely had a lot to lose. It wasn't as if most conservative Kansas families would jump up and down with joy at the news that their daughter was a lesbian—no more than her own family would if they knew the truth.

She allowed herself to remember the fear, uncertainty and self-loathing that had come with the discovery of her own sexuality. But years ago she had come to a point of acceptance, realizing that it was possible for her to have her own life and her family to have theirs. The two didn't have to be intertwined, and they didn't even have to know about hers. It was easier that way.

She hoped Jordan could come to the same conclusion, but she knew it would be a process. It had been one hell of a process for her.

Shuddering, she remembered how she had almost made her parents' dreams come true years ago. She had found a man whose company she enjoyed, and although it wasn't love, she had tried to make it so. When he had proposed, she said "yes," much to her mother's delight. She remembered how she had looked in the white dress her mother had helped her pick for her wedding day, and how for a short while, she had been okay with settling. She had been so scared of who she was that she was willing to mask it—forever. Thankfully, they hadn't gone through with it, but she had almost become the fairy tale princess replica that her parents had wanted her to be. As she thought about the road Jordan had ahead of her, Taylor hoped she wouldn't second-guess herself to that degree.

If she had learned anything over the years, it was that she didn't need to fit anyone else's mold to find her own happiness. She willed Jordan to find the same strength.

Hours passed as she sat taking in the beauty of the scenery and trying to make sense of this small-town world. When she finally decided to go back into town, she didn't have any further answers than she had before. All she knew was that she wouldn't pressure Jordan into doing anything she didn't want to do. If she wanted space and time to figure things out, Taylor would give her exactly that.

With her mind made up not to contact Jordan until she was ready, she headed back to her own house.

Evening light faded into twilight as she busied herself cleaning her house. When her phone rang, she looked at the caller ID and hesitated. Even if she wanted to, she couldn't deny her heart the chance to hear Jordan's sweet voice.

"Hey. Can I come by?"

Taylor's heart leapt, but only momentarily as she remembered that Jordan wasn't sure about continuing the intimacy they had shared. "Of course. Is everything okay?"

"I don't know."

The words cut to Taylor's heart, and she held her breath.

"I'll be over in a few minutes."

Taylor kept the phone to her ear, listening to the dead space and trying not to give into the emotional roller coaster that threatened her. She would know soon enough what was ahead for them.

Opening the door twenty minutes later, she braced herself.

"Hi," Jordan said in a small voice. Her face was devoid of any signs of readable emotion. Whatever she was feeling, she was keeping it under lock and key.

"Hey," Taylor said, stepping aside to let Jordan in the house.

Jordan seated herself on the opposite end of the couch from Taylor and sat in silence.

"Can I get you anything to drink?" Taylor asked.

"No, thank you."

The silence between them grew until Taylor broke it. "Is there any chance you want to talk about what's bothering you?" She watched as Jordan took a deep breath.

"I'm not sure what's bothering me," she admitted slowly. "Everything is so jumbled up inside of my mind, and I just want it to stop for a moment. I just want things to be clear."

"What things?" Taylor asked the question, even though she knew the answer.

"I want to know what's going on in my head and in my heart—and especially with my body." Jordan's words now tumbled out in a blur of confusion. "I feel things with you that I've never felt before, and that terrifies me."

She paused before looking Taylor directly in the eye. "It's wrong," she whispered.

The simple statement sliced through Taylor, but she managed to take it in with only a shake of her head. "It's not wrong," she said gently. "There's nothing wrong about following your heart and being with who you want to be with." She knew the words sounded cliché, like something from an after school special, but they were the truth. "I know it's a hard concept to grasp," she said, reaching over to place a supportive hand on Jordan's shoulder.

Jordan jumped back at the touch as though she had been slapped.

"Wow," Taylor said, standing up to put even more distance between them.

"I'm sorry," Jordan said. "I just don't think physical contact is best in this situation."

"Why not? You're my best friend. I can't reach out and offer you a hand of support?"

Jordan shook her head. "Not with how I feel about you, you can't. It just makes me want to do things I shouldn't do."

"Who says you shouldn't?"

Taylor knew she was playing devil's advocate contrary to her previous decision to back off, but she wanted to get through to this girl that there was so much more to the world than the narrow views of this small town.

"Everyone," Jordan said quietly. "My parents raised me to know right from wrong, and they instilled in my head that this was wrong."

"They're afraid of what they don't understand," Taylor said from the kitchen, pouring a vodka. "I get it. I was raised the same way. Do you think my dad or mom would really be on board with all this?"

She took a sip of the strong drink and took a seat on one of the barstools. "Of course they wouldn't be," she said. "They don't get it either. They're afraid of it, they don't think it's right. But what they think doesn't matter. I am who I am, and so are you. You have nothing to be ashamed of."

Taylor watched as what could only be interpreted as sheer torment passed over Jordan's face.

"I don't want to be like this," Jordan finally admitted.

The confession broke Taylor's heart. She, too, had shared a similar sentiment once upon a time.

"We don't really get a choice," Taylor said, coming to sit beside Jordan again. "But you don't have to hate it. You're a beautiful girl with a good heart. You are sweet and smart, and you should love yourself. Take all the time that you need, and I'll be here when you get it figured out."

Jordan's brow wrinkled, and she tilted her head to the side. "I just don't understand," she said.

"What don't you understand?"

"I don't understand how I can feel so conflicted. I don't understand how something can be okay if everyone says it's so wrong. I don't understand how it can be wrong when it feels so right."

Without another word, Jordan reached up and pulled Taylor to her. She pressed her lips against Taylor's and gently wove her fingers through her hair.

Taylor gave into the moment briefly and then pulled away. "I don't want to complicate things for you," she said, explaining her actions to a perplexed-looking Jordan.

"I want to feel that way again," she said. "I know I'm confused, but I want you to show me again what it's like to feel pleasure and to get lost in your arms."

Her hormones raged war against common sense, and even though she knew it was a stupid move, she let Jordan kiss her passionately once more. When Jordan pulled back and she gazed into those green eyes, she lost all control and felt her strength walk out the door.

Her love for Jordan overwhelmed her, and she straddled Jordan on the couch, kissing every inch of her body as she worked the clothes off her. When Jordan lay naked underneath her, she brought her own naked body to lay on top of Jordan's. Moving rhythmically, she listened to Jordan moan. She leaned down to kiss Jordan's neck, only to hear the moans turn into sobs.

Immediately, she stopped moving and looked down into Jordan's crying eyes.

"I can't do it," Jordan sobbed. "I'm so sorry."

Taylor nodded and kissed her on the forehead, got up and went to the bathroom to get dressed.

As she put her clothes back on, she knew she shouldn't have let herself get sucked into this again. Silently scolding herself for everything she'd done that she'd promised herself not to do, she went back out into the living room, only to find Jordan gone.

CHAPTER TWELVE

Pacing back and forth nervously in her living room, Jordan replayed her plan through her head for what felt like the millionth time.

She knew there were things that needed to be said, and at the very least she owed Taylor an explanation. While it had only been five days since she had talked to Taylor, it felt like an eternity. In the time that had passed in silence, she felt her heart grow heavier with each passing day.

Taylor was bound to think that Jordan had no feelings whatsoever for her, and that was far from the truth. She just didn't know how to handle this.

Wringing her hands, she let one final tear fall before steadying herself and preparing to have the conversation she had been dreading.

She glanced at her phone and considered calling ahead, but she was afraid Taylor wouldn't answer. These were things she needed to say in person. She grabbed her keys and headed for the door.

On the drive over, she tried to rid her mind of the memories of Taylor's kiss, but despite her best efforts her skin tingled in response to her memories.

As she pulled into the driveway, Taylor was pulling out.

"Wait," she yelled, rolling down her window and waving at Taylor. She hadn't driven all this way just to miss out on her opportunity to talk to her friend.

Taylor put the truck in park, leaving the engine running, and got out. "What's up?" she asked, all too casually, walking toward Jordan's car.

"I want to talk to you."

"Now you want to talk?" The hurt in Taylor's eyes wasn't quite masked by her sarcasm.

"Yeah," Jordan said, looking down for a second. "Do you have a few minutes?"

Taylor looked like she wanted to protest and refuse, but instead she simply nodded.

"Do you want to go inside and chat?" Jordan asked, pointing to Taylor's front door.

Taylor shook her head. "We can chat in here," she said, walking over to Jordan's passenger side and getting in the car.

Not looking at her, Jordan listened for the click of the door closing. Finally, she took a deep breath and shifted in her seat to face Taylor. "I'm sorry," she said, her voice barely above a whisper. "I'm sorry about everything."

"Me too."

"I didn't mean to hurt you or upset you, and I'm sorry that I left the other night. It was just too much to handle." She knew it was a pitiful excuse, but in all her thinking, she couldn't come up with a better reason for why she had acted so foolishly.

Taylor shrugged, and Jordan hated seeing what she had done to this girl.

"It's not that I didn't want to stay," she tried to explain. "I wanted to stay more than anything in the world. And it's not that I don't care about you or love your friendship or the things we've shared. It's that I love you—and I love the time with you—far too much for it to be okay."

She watched as Taylor took in her words, a guarded, yet wounded, look in her eyes.

"We've had the discussion about whether or not it's okay." Taylor's response sounded hollow and defeated. "But it looks like you've made up your mind."

"Can we still be friends?" Jordan asked. "I can't fathom the thought of losing you from my life completely."

"I guess that depends on a couple of factors," Taylor said with a shrug.

"What factors are those?"

"First," Taylor said with a sad smile, "if I look at you, do you see your best friend, or do you see someone who fucked you?"

At the words, Jordan felt her body shiver slightly in remembrance and in fresh anticipation.

"That's what I thought," Taylor said, noting Jordan's reaction.

In the silence that ensued, Jordan felt herself reach for Taylor's hand. Taylor took her hand in return, rubbed her fingers over Jordan's skin twice and then let go.

"But I do care about you, and I'm willing to give it a shot if that's what you want," Taylor admitted. "We can just focus on being friends, and we'll spend our time together in a public place so that you don't succumb to temptation."

Jordan couldn't explain the disappointment that flooded her heart. As scared and confused as she was, there was a sick and twisted part of her that wanted Taylor to fight for her, to make it a little more difficult. She knew that voicing such an opinion would only serve to cloud the already murky waters of their friendship, so instead she simply nodded.

When she had composed herself, she leaned over and gave Taylor a formal hug.

"I would love that," she said. "I want to be your friend."

The raw turmoil in Taylor's eyes was too much to take, so she turned away.

"I have another counseling session tomorrow," Jordan said, changing the subject.

Taylor let out a laugh, devoid of any real humor. "Sounds like one hell of a good time," she said sarcastically. "You'll have to let me know how things go."

"I don't really want to go, but I have to."

"You won't tell her about all of this, will you?" Taylor asked with a look of genuine fear displayed plainly on her face.

Jordan shook her head. This was the last thing she wanted to get out, and even though she desperately needed to talk to someone about it, she doubted Janelle was the best person to go to.

"Thank you," Taylor said quietly.

"So I guess we just go back to normal now?" Jordan asked. "I'm kind of new to how all this works."

"Yeah, so am I."

"What do you mean? I thought you'd done all this before."

"I've done this," Taylor said, motioning between the two of them. "If you're talking about dating and sleeping with women, yeah I've done that. But if you're talking about trying to fall out of love with my best friend, I've never quite done that."

"You're in love with me?" Jordan asked breathlessly, the words hitting her like a ton of bricks.

Taylor swallowed hard, hung her head, and nodded.

For a minute, Jordan couldn't speak, and when she finally did, tears were streaming down her face. "I thought I was the only one," she admitted. "That's what has made all of this so hard. It's just so quick. But you were my best friend. I already grew to love you in that capacity, and then everything else was just so electric. I fell hard, and I fell fast, and now I'm just in over my head."

"I get it," Taylor said, opening the car door. "I really do, and it'll take some time, but I'm willing to give it a try."

"Thank you."

Jordan knew the words weren't enough. She had crushed Taylor, and she watched as the broken girl climbed from her car.

"Do you want to get dinner tonight?" Jordan asked. "After my appointment, we could go get some pizza and hang out. It can be the kick off to our fresh start."

Taylor's expression was unreadable, but she nodded agreement.

"Let's shoot for seven o'clock."

"Sounds like a plan to me."

Before she pulled off, she made eye contact with Taylor one last time. "I'll see you in the office when I come in for my appointment."

Taylor forced a smile and waved, before walking back to her truck. Jordan watched in the rearview, but Taylor never cast a backward glance at her. She wasn't sure what she was expecting, but she felt completely unsettled.

* * *

Sitting on the couch, looking around Janelle's office, Jordan felt even more out of place than she had ever felt in her life.

It was as if she were in a completely new world. She waited until Janelle had settled the papers on her desk and removed her reading glasses. Once she had her notepad in hand, she cast her full attention to Jordan.

"How have you been?"

The question was simple, but it threatened to completely unravel the last bits of sanity Jordan had left. How had she been? Tumultuous was the only word that could describe her current state of mind, but she felt like that was an overshare. Janelle's eyes bored into Jordan's being, and she shifted uncomfortably under the intensity of the stare.

"I've been fine," she finally lied, feeling compelled to fill the silence.

"Just fine?"

Jordan forced a smile. "I'm good. I've been good. Things are going well."

The lies came slightly easier the second time around, but she still felt as if she had made the wrong choice in keeping today's appointment. She wasn't put together enough to lie her way through an entire inquisition session.

"Are you branching out and making new friends?"

Jordan just shook her head.

"Why not?"

"It's not really that easy, I guess. But, I have a few good friends."

It was an exaggeration. Taylor's face popped into her mind reminding her that she had one good friend, and there was potential that she might lose her.

"Who are these friends? Are they good influences?"

The question felt like a knife stabbing through her soul, but she forced a smile. "Just some friends from college," she said, dismissing the rest of the question.

"And how are you spending your time? Are you coping well with some of the depression?"

Depression. She hated the word. It sounded like a weakness.

"I'm not depressed."

"Okay, perhaps that's the wrong word," Janelle conceded. "How are you dealing with the feelings of rejection and abandonment since your departure with the basketball team?"

"I'm just fine," Jordan said a little too quickly. "I work out a lot. I hang out with my friends. I'm good."

Her mind flashed to the nights of drinking and her recent stint as a part-time lesbian, and she tried not to let her thoughts show.

Janelle nodded, making note of a few things in her notebook. Jordan's defensiveness grew, but she tried not to get agitated. Bringing her fingers to her mouth, she only noticed what she was doing as she felt a nail rip, sending pain into her finger.

Watching her like a hawk, Janelle tilted her head slightly, narrowing her eyes in focus.

"What are you nervous about?"

Jordan looked down at the couch. The question hadn't been asked in a way where she could refute the fact that she was nervous; instead, it had been a trap to snare her into saying what she didn't want to say.

"This all just feels so formal," she admitted, her eyes darting around the cold, impersonal room.

"It doesn't have to," Janelle said, rising from her desk and moving to join Jordan on the couch.

Jordan tried desperately to keep her heart from beating out of her chest. She didn't want her closer. It already felt like she was trying to pry for details from her desk. Now, it felt as if she was going to shake out details, regardless of whether Jordan offered them up or not.

"Don't be so alarmed," Janelle said, trying to soothe Jordan's nerves. "I only want to help you. You know I care about you and your family, and I only want good things for you. I want to try to help you work through this difficult time. I'm here for you. I will listen to whatever you need to talk about."

Trying to decipher if there was any hidden meaning behind the statement, Jordan looked away from her to a blank spot on the wall. Her growing and nagging desperation to share her thoughts and confusion with someone rose up inside her, but she resisted. This wasn't the time or place.

"Are you still spending time with Taylor Reeves?"

At the mention of Taylor's name, Jordan's hands started to shake. Her guilty conscience told her that somehow Janelle knew.

She gulped and nodded. "She's my friend," she said quietly.

"What do the two of you do when you spend time together?"

There was no added implication to the question, but Jordan felt her face blush crimson. She looked away in hopes that Janelle wouldn't notice, but it was too late.

"Are you ashamed of something? Don't be ashamed. You can talk to me."

With wide eyes, Jordan looked up to Janelle. In those eyes, she found a loving compassion looking back at her. It unnerved her more than she thought possible. It was easier when she could look at Janelle as an unattached figure, as her mother's friend, and as a counselor—not as someone who legitimately cared about her well-being.

In her mind, she quickly went through a list of people she trusted enough to share this secret with, but came up empty.

"Everything I say to you has to be kept confidential, right?" Jordan questioned, suddenly realizing that something bound by law was probably her safest bet.

Janelle nodded.

"That's right. It's confidential what you say in here."

The words brought a level of comfort to Jordan. Her heart kept beating heavily though, warning her that if she didn't share this dark secret, she might simply implode from the pressure.

"Okay," Jordan said slowly. "I've been into some kind of troubling behaviors lately."

She didn't make eye contact, because she couldn't bear to see the expression on Janelle's face. Still, she heard Janelle's pencil working furiously across her notepad.

"What kind of behaviors?" Janelle asked.

"I tried drinking lately, and I've been experimenting with a few things," she said. It was best to ease into this whole confession.

Janelle let the silence grow, and Jordan suddenly started to get concerned that she was taking it all the wrong way.

"Not like experimenting with drugs or anything," she added quickly. "I mean I've just been trying different ways of coping, I guess. You know, my whole life revolved around basketball, and now that I'm hanging out with a different group of people, I've been trying different things."

"Like?"

Jordan swallowed.

"I had sex for the first time recently."

The confession just slipped out. She hadn't been able to tell anyone—not even her roommate—about the loss of her virginity, and she had just done so casually in a counseling session. It made her hands shake even more.

When Janelle didn't immediately respond, Jordan made eye contact with her for the first time, surprised to find that there was less judgment than there was curiosity in her eyes.

"How did that make you feel?" she finally asked.

Jordan laughed nervously, suddenly feeling like she was a character in a bad movie. That was the line all psychologists were supposed to use.

She shrugged, unsure how to admit that it made her feel more alive than anything she had ever experienced. Sure, she had been raised to believe that premarital sex was immoral and dirty, not to mention the fact that sex with another woman was probably the worst thing she could have done. But, it hadn't made her feel that way.

"Are you happy with your decision?"

"I don't know," Jordan finally admitted. "I mean, it was wonderful and special, but I know it's supposed to be wrong."

"Supposed to be?"

Jordan glanced downward. Here she sat, in a church building, trying to rationalize sex.

"We have to remember that it's a pretty black-and-white situation, Jordan," Janelle said gently, but with authority. "It's not something we can negotiate. Everyone makes mistakes," she continued, but her voice was lost over the loudness of Jordan's thoughts.

That's exactly what she had been trying to do—negotiating. She was trying to make something right that she had been told was wrong.

In the light of her discovery, she looked back up to find Janelle waiting expectantly for a reply.

"I'm sorry," she said, realizing she had no clue what the question was. "What did you say?"

Janelle offered a sad smile. "I asked who you slept with."

Jordan looked away quickly. She had promised Taylor she wouldn't say anything, and even she wasn't ready to admit that much. She shook her head in response.

"Was it a boyfriend? Do you have a boyfriend?"

Jordan shook her head, complete and utter fear seeping through every part of her body. She knew she had said too much, and she watched in horror as Janelle's eyes widened in realization and understanding.

For a minute, neither of them spoke. Janelle was obviously taking in the unspoken news, and Jordan was too terrified to speak. This was all new to her, and she hadn't wanted anyone to find out. But, at the same time, she felt a slight bit of relief that someone knew. Maybe Janelle could help her deal with this. After all, she was a counselor. That was her job.

Finally, she forced herself to make eye contact again.

"Was she...was she the first woman you've felt this way about?"

Jordan didn't know how to answer that question. "I think so," she said, dismissing the reminders that those feelings had been present long before Taylor. Taylor had simply awakened them and breathed life into her desires.

"Okay, we can work to combat this," Janelle said quickly. "Let me do some research, but I think what you need most is accountability right now. Where did this encounter take place?"

Jordan's thoughts filled with the "encounters" as Janelle had called them.

When she didn't answer, Janelle pressed. "Was it at your place?"

Jordan nodded. It was best to try to keep Taylor out of trouble as much as possible.

"And do you not have a roommate?"

"I do," Jordan said. "But she's never home."

"So it was usually just the two of you at your house?"

Jordan sighed and nodded. "Yes, it was."

"Well, then, I think you need to stay somewhere else for a little while, with someone who knows what's going on and can keep you accountable."

Jordan tried to take in the statement, but she wasn't quite clear on what Janelle meant. The wheels in her head started turning, and there was only one logical explanation.

"Do you mean I should stay with you?"

Janelle nodded solemnly. "Yes, I think that's best."

It was the worst idea Jordan had ever heard, and she searched her brain for a polite way to decline. "I don't really want to," she finally managed.

"I'm not sure you have a choice," Janelle said firmly.

"What on earth do you mean I don't have a choice?" Jordan heard her own voice rise and fought to keep it in check. "I can keep myself accountable."

"Well, you haven't been doing the best job of that. Have you?"

It felt like a slap in the face, and Jordan stood, ready to leave the room. She couldn't believe she had trusted this woman.

"Jordan, go ahead and sit back down." Janelle's tone was condescending, and Jordan immediately disliked where this was headed. She should have never come here today. Trying to keep Janelle appeased, she sat back down on the couch and attempted to keep her anger at bay. Janelle was the keeper of her biggest secret, so it would serve her well to at least be polite.

"I don't want to do that," Jordan explained as calmly as she possibly could. "I'm a grown woman. I can control my own life."

Janelle narrowed her eyes. "Just for two weeks, you stay with me. I'll make sure you don't spend any time with Taylor, and we'll work on getting you the help you need."

Jordan shook her head adamantly.

"What's the problem? Do you still want to see her?"

The question was a loaded one, and Jordan could see the trap being set.

"I just want to try to sort through this on my own."

"No, you don't," Janelle said, casually as if she were explaining a choice on a dinner menu. "You don't want to handle it alone, or you wouldn't have come to me. You're seeking help, whether you can see it or not. And, if you let me help you, we can make sure no one else knows about this. If not, I'll have to involve your parents."

The threat resonated within her. She had confessed sleeping with Taylor to her mother's best friend. Fresh fear flooded her veins.

"Don't tell my parents," she begged. "I don't want them—or anyone else—to find out about this. Please."

"Your secret is safe with me as long as you allow me to help you."

Jordan wasn't sure which was stronger—her anger at Janelle or her fear of her parents finding out the truth about their little girl. As she sat on the couch, she realized that her fear was going to win out.

"What do I have to do?"

"Stay with me. Stay away from Taylor. And let me help you."

"Three simple steps," Jordan said sarcastically, knowing on the inside that they were the last three things on earth that she wanted to do.

"I can help you," Janelle assured her.

The words were what Jordan had been longing to hear—that there was some sort of help for her. She didn't want to be this way, even though it was something she could see that she had clearly been struggling with for quite some time.

"Can I at least talk to her and let her know first?"

Janelle's eyes narrowed, but she nodded. "If you must. But, be at my house by no later than six o'clock tonight, or I'll have to call your parents."

She wanted to protest. What was said in this room was supposed to be confidential. Janelle had promised as much, but now that she was the bearer of Jordan's secret, she held the power. Jordan nodded and wiped the tear that threatened to fall.

Without another word, she gathered her purse and headed out of the office.

"Six o'clock," Janelle reminded before she shut the door.

On the way out, she passed by Taylor's desk. "Can I speak with you outside?" she asked quietly, careful not to disturb anyone else in the office.

Taylor looked up, a million questions in her eyes. She glanced around to make sure they hadn't attracted the attention of anyone else and nodded. "I'll be right out," she whispered. "Just give me a minute."

Jordan walked out of the office, unsure how she was going to tell Taylor what she needed to say. There was no doubt she would feel betrayed, and rightfully so. But, in reality, Jordan hadn't really offered any sort of confession. She had just stated some facts, and Janelle had connected the dots.

Taylor's minute seemed to take forever, and Jordan fretted in her car, wishing she could just disappear from this town.

When she saw Taylor approaching her car, every muscle in her body tensed. This was something they never quite prepared anyone for.

Taylor opened the passenger door and climbed inside. "What's up?" she asked.

Jordan opened her mouth to speak, but nothing came out. Instead, tears flooded from her eyes. "I can't see you anymore—at least not for a while." The words were choked out through tears.

"What do you mean?" Taylor asked skeptically. "You told her, didn't you?"

"Not really," Jordan tried to explain. "She guessed. She put the pieces together. I don't know. I didn't say anything about you. She just guessed."

"And when she guessed, you didn't think to deny it?"

The question came out more like an accusation, and Jordan wanted to get defensive. "I started crying," she said. "This isn't easy for me, okay? I didn't want to tell her anything. I'm just trying to process it all, and it's a little hard on my own."

Taylor shook her head, the raw emotion warring in her eyes, threatening to let tears fall in the place of the anger that she had put up as a guard wall. Her hands shook as she spoke, and Jordan could see that there was a slow-burning temper laying just below the calm demeanor that Taylor always presented. "Now that she knows, everyone is going to know. I should just leave town so my parents don't have to deal with this."

"No!" Jordan's plea came out in a near scream. "Please don't leave."

"Why not? You can't see me anyway, remember?"

"That's only for two weeks. She made me promise to stay away for two weeks, or she's going to tell my parents."

When Taylor didn't respond, she continued. "Besides, she said she can help me. Then, we can be friends and go back to normal."

"It doesn't work like that," Taylor said as tears began to roll down her cheeks. "It just doesn't. I love you. You love me. It's not like you can go through some kind of weird therapy and then it all just goes back to normal. Love doesn't work like that."

Jordan felt as if her heart was being torn to shreds with each word. "I would be with you in a heartbeat if things were different," she said, wishing that things could be different somehow.

"But, they're not," Taylor said, stiffening in the passenger seat.

"I do love you."

"I love you too," Taylor said, obviously defeated. She let out a long sigh. "Look, Jordan, here's the deal. You go and do your therapy thing. You take your time, and if you want to talk to me after all the awful things she'll tell you about me, give me a call."

"Of course I'll want to talk to you. Staying away from you these last couple of days has been the hardest thing I've ever done. I can't be without you."

"Well then, I guess you have your answer," Taylor said.

Leaning over, she got inches from Jordan's lips. A faint smile flashed over Taylor's mouth, before she pressed her lips to Jordan's.

After a passionate and steamy kiss, Taylor pulled back. "I had to," she said. "It was either a goodbye kiss, or an 'I'll see you in two weeks' kiss."

As Taylor got out of the car, Jordan wasn't sure what to do. Her lips still burned from the kiss, and she couldn't deny that she wanted more. But, she couldn't have more—especially not right now.

After going home and packing some necessary items, she knew there was no way she was going to get that kiss out of her mind. Nor was there any way she could ignore the pained expression on Taylor's face.

Back in her car, she looked in the rearview mirror, gazing at the haunted eyes that stared back at her that seemed no longer her own. They were the eyes of someone who had aged overnight—of someone who had finally tasted love and had had it ripped away by the cruelties of the world.

There was no doubt she could have what she wanted, if only she would give in. But it wasn't right, and she didn't want to be that weak. She would be strong, and she would give this a legitimate shot.

She owed herself that much.

Thinking once more of Taylor's kiss, she got out of the car and walked up the steps to Janelle's house. With a sinking feeling, she knew she was sacrificing her freedom—and perhaps her only shot at a love that strong—all to save face and her relationship with her family.

She reached up to knock on the door, hoping it was worth it. Before she could knock, the door swung open.

Janelle appeared in the doorway, looking overexcited about her new houseguest—her latest project, no doubt. Jordan stifled a sigh.

"I saw you pull up," Janelle explained quickly. "Come on in, and let's get started."

"It's been a long day," Jordan said. "Can I just get some sleep and we can work on things tomorrow?"

Janelle looked disappointed but quickly recovered. "Of course," she said, stepping aside so Jordan could enter. "I'll show you where to put your things."

She led Jordan down a small hallway to a corner bedroom. "This is our spare bedroom. It's all yours for the time you're staying here, and the bathroom is down the hall to the right."

Jordan couldn't help but feel like she had been checked into a mental institution, but then again, she had heard her father talk about homosexuals as if it were a mental disease, so maybe she was in the right place.

She thanked Janelle and closed the door to the bedroom. It was hot, and she wanted to escape out the window. If she did, though, there was no doubt where she would end up. She would race as quickly as she could until she was back in Taylor's arms.

Lying back on the bed, she couldn't help but see the next two weeks as a prison sentence. She pulled out her cell phone and, despite her better judgment, typed out a text to Taylor.

I love you. Just wanted you to know.

It was simple, but it got the point across.

She knew she shouldn't, but she hit send before she could talk herself out of it. She dropped the phone when she heard an abrupt knock on the door. More than anything, she wanted to ignore the knock, but she knew she couldn't.

"Come in," she said softly.

Janelle opened the door and peeked inside.

"I just wanted to give you the few simple rules," she said, entering the room and shutting the door behind her. "My family doesn't know why you're here. They just know that you needed a little extra help. I'd prefer to keep it that way—for your sake and mine."

"Okay," Jordan said. There was no way in hell she was going to divulge that information to anyone—let alone Janelle's family members.

"Also, I'll give you the Wi-Fi code, on one condition."

Jordan shrugged. Right now, she didn't care about Internet connection, but it might come in handy during her prison sentence.

"What's the condition?" Jordan finally asked.

"You don't use it to contact Taylor," she said matter-of-factly. "I'll be asking you periodically if you've talked to her, and I'm good enough at reading people that I'll know if you're lying. If you aren't committed to letting me help you—and if you end up lying to me or contacting her—I'll have to tell your parents."

Jordan resisted the urge to call her a power-hungry bitch and run out the door. Instead, she sat seething in her anger.

"This is only because I care about you and want to see you get better. I care about you and your family, and I know that they would want the same for you. You just don't want to tell them, so I'm forced to step in and help where they can't."

Janelle wasn't being forced to do anything. Jordan was. They both knew it, and Jordan hated the way she was playing the victim in this mess.

"Fine," Jordan finally said, conceding.

"Good," Janelle said. "The only other rule is that you can't text or call Taylor. It won't help you, and it will only confuse you more and further complicate the situation."

Jordan felt as if she had been caught red-handed. It was as if Janelle was watching her every move.

Unfortunately, it was at that exact moment that her phone beeped beside her, signaling an incoming text message. Jordan froze and quickly reached for the phone.

"Who is it?" Janelle asked.

Jordan shot her a look, asking her to back off silently.

Janelle narrowed her eyes at Jordan. "Who is it?" she asked again.

With a frustrated sigh, Jordan looked down at the phone.

There in simple wording was the message that she needed to hear.

I love you too, J. Talk to you soon.

"It was no one," Jordan said, shutting the text and holding onto her phone tightly.

"Was it Taylor?" Janelle asked pointedly.

"Fine, it was Taylor," Jordan admitted. "It was a goodbye text."

"It better have been," Janelle said, and turned on her heel.

As she rose from the bed and shut the door behind her, Jordan clutched her phone to her chest and let her tears fall silently. Never had she felt more alone.

She couldn't help but feel like her spirit was being crushed, like she was slowly losing the parts of her strength and confidence she valued most. As she cried, she let her thoughts drift back to one of the best days she had spent with Taylor.

Whoosh.

The sound of a basketball slicing through the net made Jordan feel more alive than she had felt in a long time.

"Nice shot!" Taylor shouted, rebounding the ball and tossing it back to her for another shot.

Jordan squared her feet and sank another shot.

"Why did you stop coming out here again?" Taylor asked, somewhat breathless from continually chasing down the ball so that Jordan didn't have to cut and jump too quickly for her knee to bear.

"It got too hard," Jordan admitted as she continued to do what felt most natural to her.

For as long as she could remember, catching and shooting repeatedly had been one of the most therapeutic exercises anytime she was upset or needed to work through her thoughts.

"You're stronger than that," Taylor said, holding the ball on her hip.

"Just throw me the ball," Jordan said, not wanting to hear a life lesson.

Taylor shook her head, refusing to let Jordan move on from the moment without addressing the deeper roots of her problem. "You're stronger than you give yourself credit for being," Taylor said, walking toward Jordan. She cupped Jordan's face in her hands and looked deep into her eyes. "You're probably one of the strongest people I've ever met, and you keep selling yourself short. Don't give up on something you love just because you think the path is going to be hard—or even painful."

Jordan looked away, feeling the words slice through her heart.

"No, you will never play basketball again on an official team, but that doesn't mean you have to give up on something that brings you so much joy. Keep doing your rehabilitation exercises, keep practicing, and play on an intramural league. You'll kick some ass and feel better."

"I don't want to play anymore," Jordan said angrily, grabbing the ball from where Taylor had sat it on the ground.

"Why not?"

It was a simple question, but one that Jordan wasn't willing to address.

"It won't be the same," she finally answered. "And I might not be as good."

Taylor's gaze cut into her soul, and she felt the need to continue.

"More than anything, I just don't play—or even come out to this court anymore—because it reminds me of all that I had, all that I lost, all that I'll never have again."

"Things are always going to change," Taylor declared, "but that doesn't mean you'll never have it again. It will just be different, but it will still be the game that you love. Fight for yourself a little bit more, Jordan. I believe in you."

Jordan had looked away, but she let the words resonate within her spirit. Taylor believed in her and thought she was strong. While she had always thought she was strong, that feeling had been somewhat stripped in recent months.

"Don't forget how strong you are," Taylor *had whispered before hugging Jordan and walking away to grab a bottle of water.*

As Jordan sat in the empty room, she again heard Taylor's final whisper.

She wouldn't forget how strong she was, and once she figured out what she wanted—and what she loved—she was confident that this time she would fight for herself.

For the time being, though, she had no idea what she really wanted or needed.

CHAPTER THIRTEEN

After a quick stop at a convenience store for a soda, Taylor put on her oversized sunglasses and hit the road.

She couldn't stay in this tiny town—not this weekend, not when all she wanted to do was go kick down Janelle's door and demand that she stop playing such wicked little games with an innocent like Jordan.

Sure, Jordan was easily led. Scared people always were. It was a tactic used by many—from dictators to those conducting the types of therapy Taylor was sure Janelle wanted to practice on Jordan.

She shuddered at the thought of "anti-gay" therapy. It was such a small-minded notion, and one that she would never have willingly submitted to, but this was Jordan's decision. For what felt like the hundredth time, she had to remind herself that she couldn't save Jordan. That would have to be her own doing, should she choose it.

For now, Taylor was going to make herself scarce.

With each passing mile, she felt the magnetic pull and could almost physically feel the pain of leaving Jordan behind in that awful place. More than anything, she wanted to take Jordan with her, but that was impossible.

Trying to channel her inner optimism, she refused to cry. Still, the reality was crushing. At this very moment, a meddling counselor was attempting to cure Jordan of her love for Taylor, and Jordan was willingly allowing it. The truth of the matter was that Jordan wanted to be cured.

Taylor's heart fell again as she replayed that truth over and over in her mind. A sudden feeling of hopelessness flooded her entire being, and she feared that there would come a day when Jordan wouldn't even want to see her, let alone love her.

She couldn't explain her intense connection to the girl, but she knew that it would be the hardest thing she would ever get over.

Turning up her music as loud as it would go, she decided that would be the goal of this weekend away. After all, she was going back to the one place she felt at home. Out of all the places she had lived, only Oklahoma was home.

Determined to put it all behind her, she watched the landscape as the miles passed. The golden wheat fields of rural Kansas caught the sunlight and gave her a glint of hope. Each small town and city had its unique buildings and people milling around, all reminding her that everyone had their own story. As she crossed into Oklahoma and cattle filled the pastures along the side of the road, she took comfort in the fact that these were familiar roads, and she was on her way home. Nonetheless, she couldn't deny that her heart was at war with her mind. While she wasn't sure she wanted to forget and move on, she knew good and well that it was probably her only chance at escaping with a shred of sanity left.

Pretty girls were always the downfall of an otherwise smart and strong person, she reflected. It seemed that the pretty, smart, and funny ones, however, might just be the cause of sheer insanity.

As dusk fell, and the air cooled down somewhat, Taylor rolled down the windows to drink in some of the fresh, country air. Although it smelled of cattle and alfalfa hay, she relished it as though it was a long-lost friend.

When she finally pulled into her old friend's driveway, she sat for a minute, remembering life before Jordan. Lately it seemed like everything had spiraled out of control. Ever since that beauty walked into her life, she had been upside down and inside out. Even now her thoughts drifted away to those green eyes and those soft lips—and the tenderness with which they caressed Taylor's own lips. She sighed, pushing the thoughts away.

Back home, she knew the hammer was about to drop, and she didn't want to be anywhere near when it did. This was no time for her superhero complex to come roaring in to save the day. Nor was it any time to look her parents in the eye and see their disappointment and judgment. It was simply the time for a little bit of rest, relaxation, and remembering what was important in life.

Before she could get out of the truck, she saw her oldest friend Amy bound down the steps of the house, her blond hair blowing in the breeze, fully capturing her free-spirited approach to life that had initially bonded them so closely as kids. When she was in plain view, Taylor could see the smile spread across her face. Even though a year had passed since they had seen each other, nothing had changed. Amy didn't look a day over twenty-three, and she looked genuinely happy. For a brief second, Taylor envied that.

"Taylor!" she exclaimed, bringing a smile to Taylor's face. "I'm so happy to see you," she added, opening the driver's side door before Taylor could do so herself.

Taylor was about to share the sentiment when a look of concern clouded Amy's eyes.

"What's wrong?"

Right there, suddenly feeling the support system she had been missing, Taylor felt tears stream from her eyes. Without missing a beat, Amy wrapped her arms around Taylor's shoulders. "What is it? You can talk to me."

Taylor knew that Amy was telling the truth and not simply feeding her empty words, but she couldn't put what she needed to say in words just yet. Instead, she shook her head. "We'll talk later," she promised. "For now, let's get an umbrella drink in this hand and some party lights out on the patio."

Amy smiled, and nodded. "Whatever you need, you've got it. We'll get you back to your old self in no time at all."

Taylor smiled, but she knew it looked forced. There was no way to explain to Amy that she would never be her old self again. No matter how brief their relationship had been, Jordan had left her mark on Taylor's heart. She had come in and shaken up her world, and Taylor knew she would never be the same again.

She grabbed her bag and followed her bubbly blond friend out to the patio. If there was a cure for the hurt she felt, she would find it here.

For the time being, she needed to try to forget what it was like to love Jordan Weston, and a few minutes later, as she felt the sting of the rum in the back of her throat, she could think of no more fitting way to drown her sorrows than with alcohol.

* * *

Water splashed out of the pot onto the stove. A sizzling sound filled the room. Janelle fought the urge to curse out loud. She wasn't sure why she was trying so hard to impress this girl, but she wanted her to at least feel at home and be well fed. As she cooked, she tried to ignore the look of disgust on the girl's face.

To say the air between them was tense would be a gross understatement. She recalled the fire with which Jordan usually spoke and the passion with which she lived her life. Now she was nothing but the defeated and angry shell of the girl she had once been. That would have to change.

It was best if her clients—or projects as her son called them—felt at ease. As it was, though, Jordan looked like she either wanted to vomit or run away from the house screaming.

Hoping to avoid both options, Janelle cleared her throat. "How are you doing?" The question came out sounding flat, but it was the best she could do.

Jordan looked at Janelle, her eyes full of darkness, and merely shrugged. It was the type of expression that would have driven any half-decent parent mad, but she took a deep breath, reminding herself that this was not her child.

"Are you settling into your room? Do you need anything else?" She knew she was just desperately reaching for some kind of response from the girl, but again Jordan just silently gestured.

With a shake of her head, she said everything she needed to say. The silent "fuck off" was as clear as if Jordan had shouted it throughout the house.

Turning her attention back to the stove, she decided she would try again later. Perhaps after a meal and a little time to herself, Jordan would be ready to talk. Then, Janelle could ask the necessary questions and begin the therapy that she knew needed to take place.

There was no way that she was going to let this sweet girl succumb to the evils of the homosexual lifestyle. Her parents had raised her better than that, and Janelle wasn't going to stand by and watch someone as vile as Taylor Reeves suck Jordan into a lifestyle of sin.

She straightened her shoulders and slid the noodles further into the water. The entire time, she could feel Jordan's eyes boring holes into the back of her head. It was an eerie feeling, similar to what a gazelle must feel as the lion stalked it prior to devouring it.

The front door opened and slammed shut, and she saw Trevor blaze into the kitchen. "Hey Mom," he shouted, his voice far too happy for his typical behavior.

For a moment, she wondered if her son had come back to her. Then she couldn't help the doubt that settled into her brain. Maybe he had just found some happier drugs to take. She hated herself for having the thoughts, but she knew that there had to be some sort of explanation, and he hadn't exactly been in the business of making it easy to trust him lately.

"Hey Trev," she said. "Go wash up and let's have some dinner."

Trevor scanned the room to see what was for dinner, before spotting Jordan sitting at the table. Completely ignoring his mom's request, he sidled up to the table. "Hi," he said, his voice suddenly both deeper and softer. "How have you been, Jordan? I haven't really seen you recently, aside from church stuff."

Jordan gave him a smile, but it was obviously out of sheer politeness and devoid of any interest. "I'm good. It's good to see you."

Trevor's smile grew as he pulled out a chair and sat beside her. "You're staying for dinner, I hope."

Janelle fought the urge to laugh at her son's shameless flirting and willingness to invite anyone to dinner without checking with her first. In this case, she was glad, though. It had been a different story when he was a child and would bring anyone and everyone over for dinner. Now, she watched out of the corner of her eye as Jordan nodded. Her eyes showed signs of defeat, and she was quickly caving to Janelle's plan. It would be better this way. Soon, Jordan would see.

Trevor chatted with ease, seeming not to notice how little Jordan gave in response. Janelle listened quietly, hoping that maybe this type of interaction would be beneficial for Jordan. If Trevor could get her to open up and talk a little bit, it would make Janelle's therapy easier. Similarly, maybe Jordan would be good for Trevor to bring him out of the angst-filled teenage behavior he had been exhibiting.

She tried to ignore them and focus on the task at hand. There were so many things she had read about but never had to try. Homosexuals just weren't that common in her circle of clients, so this was going to take her full attention.

Finishing up the dinner preparations, she glanced over to the table to find Trevor completely mesmerized by everything Jordan was saying. Truth be told, she wasn't saying much. But at least she was making progress, reliving her knee injury for his entertainment.

He hung on every word she said, and Janelle saw an attentiveness in his eyes that she hadn't seen in years. The sight gave her a small bit of hope. It meant he hadn't lost interest in all things. Instead, he was just a teenage boy with an adoration for getting high and a lack of interest in anything his mother condoned.

Quizzically, she eyed them, assessing the situation. They were only a couple of years apart in age, and if she played her cards right, maybe she could work some magic there. It was no doubt that Trevor needed a good, strong girl in his life, and Jordan needed a man—any man to make her forget about Taylor.

"Dinner is ready," she said, reluctantly breaking up the moment by setting the spaghetti on the table.

"Thanks, Mom," Trevor said.

Janelle laughed. This was obviously part of the show he was putting on for Jordan's sake. She couldn't remember the last time he had thanked her for anything. In fact, last time she had made spaghetti, he had refused to eat.

Shaking her head, she took a seat and watched as he dished some first for Jordan and then some for himself. Jordan squirmed uncomfortably in her chair, accepting the plate of food with as much tact as possible.

Unable to take her silent disgust any longer, Janelle cleared her throat. "Is something wrong?" The question was more pointed than she had intended, so she did her best to offer a smile to soften the blow.

Jordan shook her head. "Thank you for dinner," she said, sounding more like a petulant child than a grown adult.

In that moment, Janelle wanted to wring her neck. Of course, the situation was less than ideal, but if this girl couldn't understand that Janelle was simply trying to help, they were going to have issues. "You're welcome," she said finally, scooping up the noodles with her fork.

Trevor continued to make small talk until he had scarfed down his dinner in nothing flat.

"I've got to go," he said, looking at the clock on the wall. "But will you be around later?"

Jordan let out a small, sad laugh. "Yeah, I'll be here."

"Cool."

With that, Trevor was gone, not even acknowledging his mother's presence again. For what felt like the millionth time, she thought about chasing him down and telling him to at least ask permission to leave, but she didn't want to appear weak in front of Jordan. Besides, he had long ago established that if she refused to let him go, he'd sneak out. He was her biggest losing battle, and his stubborn nature showed no signs of ever wavering. She had done him no favors by giving him the authority in their relationship, but she wanted his love more than she wanted control. She pushed the thoughts away, focusing on the situation at hand. Trevor was fond of this houseguest, that much was certain. Some of the others she had brought home over the years had not gone over so well. She could remember him begging her to leave her job at work, but it wasn't that simple—especially when it was the daughter of one of her oldest friends. With Trevor gone, she knew it was time to break the ice.

She let out a deep breath and then pushed her plate aside. "Is something wrong with the food?" Janelle asked, noting that Jordan hadn't taken even a single bite.

Jordan shook her head. "I'm not really crazy about spaghetti."

"You should have said something."

Jordan sighed slightly. "It doesn't matter," she said. "I'm not hungry anyway." She pushed the plate away and looked down at the table.

"Do you want to share with me what you're feeling?" Janelle invited.

"Not really."

"Can you try?"

Jordan's forehead wrinkled as if she was trying to pick her words carefully. "I feel like hell," she suddenly blurted out. "I feel trapped. I feel like I'm a mess. I don't want to be this way, but at the same time, I don't want to be held hostage and forced to stop contacting my best friend."

"You're still holding on to her, I see," Janelle noted disapprovingly.

"What?" Jordan's voice was incredulous.

"I mean, you're still calling her your best friend. You obviously haven't let go of anything the way you should have."

"You have no idea what it's like to be in love, do you?"

Jordan's simple question shot a barb through her heart. Once upon a time, she had known. Now, she wasn't so certain.

Janelle straightened in her chair and narrowed her eyes at Jordan. If this girl was going to get the point, she was going to have to be more blunt and forthcoming. "I may not understand what the two of you had," she said, trying to keep her tone even despite her boiling blood. "But I know it wasn't love. I know that you are just a young girl who got caught up in a bad situation. You made some bad choices. You fell into sin, and now it's time for you to make a choice to lead a better life."

"Taylor and I are somehow lesser. Is that what you're saying?"

Janelle cleared her throat again. Jordan wasn't going to make this easy. She had always been a stubborn child.

"I'm not saying you're any less than anyone else. I'm simply saying that what you and Taylor had was wrong. Plain and simple. It's black-and-white. There is no gray area. It's wrong. You can't be with another woman. I forbid you to do that."

She watched as the storm of anger brewed in Jordan's eyes, and she knew she had crossed a line. Jordan was not her daughter. It was not her place to forbid her from anything. But at the same time, she was the girl's only accountability for the time being.

"Unless you want to tell your parents, you follow my rules," she said with a shrug. "It's your choice. You need help, and I'm willing to give you the help and guidance you need so that you don't have to go to them with this problem. If you fight it, though, or if you decide the rules need to be broken, I'll have to tell them."

"I don't need guidance," Jordan argued. "I'm fine. I just need to do this on my own."

"Doing things on your own got you into this mess, and into Taylor Reeves's bed."

She watched for the obvious signs of torment to come up at the mention of Taylor's name. As they always did, Jordan's eyes almost filled with tears at the name.

"We're going to get through this," Janelle said, reaching across the table to grab Jordan's hand.

Jordan's body stiffened and the steeled look in her eyes signified that she wanted to pull back, but she relented.

"You don't want to be a lesbian, do you?" she asked.

In response, the tears that had pooled slid down Jordan's cheek, and she shook her head. "No," she said quietly. "I don't."

"What do you want?"

"I want to be normal. I want to find a love that I can have. But more than anything, I want my best friend here to talk to me about all of this."

"You can't have that," Janelle said, lowering her voice for dramatic effect. "But you can pray. That will help more than anything."

Jordan let out a sigh, but she nodded. Looking like a sad little girl, she cleared her plate and walked to her room with slumped shoulders.

This was only the beginning, but Janelle was confident that she could make life better for Jordan. After washing the dishes, she retreated to her own bedroom and picked up the textbooks she had been reading. All of them promised that it wasn't an easy cure, but that homosexuality could be overcome. She was determined to prove that theory right. Thumbing through one of the books, she looked through the simpler methods—everything from prayer to negative associations. Those would be useful, but she had a feeling Jordan was far too stubborn to be an easy fix. She flipped through the pages that were labeled for extreme cases. If she was going to try to fix Taylor, those would be necessary—but, thankfully Taylor was not her problem.

Glancing at them in case they were needed later on, she shuddered slightly. Electrotherapy didn't quite sound like something she should ever attempt to practice, but the book was decades old. With her mind reeling, she earmarked the pages she felt were most important. Feelings of guilt threatened to rise to the surface, but she pushed them down, shaking her head and reminding herself that it was her responsibility to help this poor girl find her way again. And, she would do whatever it took to accomplish the task.

CHAPTER FOURTEEN

Wind whipped through the curtained windows, and a soothing song played through the speakers of her phone, but it wasn't enough to calm Jordan's nerves. She felt like she had been physically beaten. Her head pounded, and her entire body felt shaky. Even though she tried to focus, she knew she was really doing nothing but mindlessly flipping through the pages of her book. With a sigh, she shut the book and sat back on the bed. Thoughts rolled through her mind rapidly, like an ever-changing flashing sign. The thunderstorm brewing outside held no advantage in tenacity over her conflicting emotions. She looked around, hating every detail of this room, hating even more the fact that she felt like a prisoner here.

Dread filled her and weighed her down as she thought about what would surely lay ahead of her this evening. There would be more questions. There were always so many questions—some of which she felt as if she needed to lie about.

Of course she still had feelings for Taylor, even if they were feelings she couldn't explain. Yet, if she ever answered that way,

Janelle looked at her with such disgust that she felt dirty. For what felt like the hundredth time in days, she gave in to tears.

All day, she had longed for some sort of normalcy to her life. Even more, she had wanted to hear from Taylor. She would have taken anything—a text message, a phone call, or even something as simple as passing her car on the street. She had even taken the long way back to the house, hoping to see Taylor's truck parked at the church, but it was nowhere to be found. It was worrisome to her, but she knew there was no one she could ask. It was a helpless feeling, one that threatened to overtake her completely.

Against the advice she had been given, she began to let her mind wander. Janelle had instructed time and time again that she was to stop her thoughts of Taylor, that it was unhealthy to continue trying to figure out what had happened and why it happened. Instead, it was best if she just accepted that what she had done was wrong, and work to move on.

But, that wasn't good enough. It never would be.

She settled back against the pillow and let the thoughts wash over her. She saw Taylor standing there before her, bright blue eyes burning with lust, telling her truths that she already knew about herself. Her long hair curled to perfection and her lips giving Jordan a "come here" smile as she stood, long legs exposed, wearing only a black lace bra and boy shorts. For what felt like the millionth time, Jordan thought about Taylor's voice and how it would sound when Taylor told her that she wanted her. Its slight raspy nature made Jordan weak in the knees, as did thought about any part of Taylor's anatomy—especially her large breasts. Remembering how it felt to have them slide up and down her body, her breathing deepened.

She was undeniably and hopelessly attracted to Taylor Reeves and found it damn near impossible to stay away from her. Like a moth to a flame, the lure was far too powerful to combat. Even now, she let her thoughts focus on those eyes and that smile, and it was almost as if she could feel the caress of Taylor's long, slender fingers across her body and feel Taylor's body crashing against her own.

Lost in lust, she shivered and felt her body tighten. There was no denying the fact that a simple longing gaze from Taylor could set her body afire. Feeling the sensations from her fantasy overtake her, she realized all too quickly that she was tense and wet, ready to feel Taylor's touch again. She knew that a single touch to any part of her body would send her into a full explosion.

Forcing her eyes wide open, she sat upright. She would have to get a grip on these emotions sooner or later. But, despite Janelle's attempts at therapy, she was pretty sure the fight was futile.

If Taylor Reeves was the death of her, she might just have to die.

Shaking her head, she knew she was being dramatic, but she didn't care. She missed her best friend, she missed the only love she had ever known, and she was almost certain she would do anything in that moment just to have her back.

Still, she would follow the rules for the time being. There was no sense in allowing Janelle to ruin her life and her reputation just for the sake of selfish pleasure. No. She would adhere to this absurd plan, and then when she was free, she would make her own decisions—even if she was scared of what those might be.

Her cell phone rang, thankfully bringing her out of the pity party she was throwing for herself.

Quickly, she moved across the bed and grabbed it from the side table with hope that it might be Taylor. When it wasn't, she let out a sigh and chided herself for being such a girl. She forced a smile so that she wouldn't sound so down on the phone and answered it.

"Hey, Jenna," she said, attempting to keep her voice upbeat.

"Hey, roomie," Jenna said. "Is everything okay?"

"Why wouldn't it be?"

"I just stopped by the apartment, and it looks like you haven't been home in a while."

Jordan wanted to ask how she could tell, but she decided against it. "I've just been out running some errands," she lied. "I'll probably be back by later."

"Okay," Jenna conceded. "Are you sure everything is all right? I haven't seen you in a couple of weeks."

Jordan fought the urge to let Jenna know that the distance that had developed in their friendship wasn't her fault. "I know. I've missed you."

It was true. She would have given anything to have a friend she could talk to right now. But that didn't seem to be a possibility.

"I've missed you too. I won't be here when you get back later, but we'll do dinner soon."

It was an empty promise, and Jordan knew as much, but she went along with it easily enough. She let Jenna ramble on for a few minutes about the recent happenings in her life. For someone who seemed to care so much about whether or not Jordan was okay, she had forgotten all about the fact that Jordan even had a life.

Jordan let her talk because if nothing else, it was a welcome distraction. For the first time in days, something felt normal. This had been the basis of their friendship. Jenna talked. She listened. It worked for them.

When she finally hung up, she felt a little better. She glanced at the clock. There was still an hour before Janelle would be home, so she set about her homework with renewed determination. One way or another, she was going to survive her stay here.

The time passed quickly as she busied herself in work. For a little while, she forgot where she was and the crazy circumstances that had become her reality. Instead, she remembered the days when she was nothing more than a focused student. Channeling that strength, she read until she heard the front door swing open.

Closing her eyes, she took a deep breath and put a smile on her face. If Janelle wanted progress, she was going to show her progress. She straightened up on the bed and tucked her feet under her knees, sitting upright as she continued to read and pretending like she didn't even know Janelle had arrived.

Keeping her posture neutral and unalarmed, she tried to ignore the chill that went through her entire body as Janelle approached her open bedroom door. Without even looking, she knew that she was the recipient of an icy and judgmental look.

Instead of greeting her, Janelle simply cleared her throat as if commanding authority.

"Hey," Jordan said casually, finally peeling her eyes away from the book. "How was work?"

Janelle raised one eyebrow. "It was good," she said with a slight curiosity in her tone. "You seem to be in better spirits."

Jordan shrugged, trying to play it cool. "I've just been doing some reading and taking care of some stuff."

"Good," Janelle said with a nod. The hint of skepticism still hung in the air between them. "Have you talked to Taylor?"

"No."

Janelle stepped closer to the bed to look Jordan directly in the eye. "Have you texted her? Has she texted you? Has there been any communication?"

Jordan bit her tongue, fighting off the sarcastic replies that threatened to shoot out of her mouth. "No, there has not," she replied finally.

"Good. Then, let's get to work, if you're ready."

Jordan gave herself a silent pep talk. The sooner they did this, the sooner it would be over, and then she could try to sort through the thoughts in her head on her own. She was certain that was the only way she was going to be able to deal with this ordeal, but Janelle was persistent and devious with her blackmail schemes.

"I'm ready," she finally said, her voice sounding foreign even to her own ears.

Something had changed in her over the course of her so-called therapy, and she didn't like it. Nonetheless, she followed Janelle down the hall to the study.

Without having to be asked, she took a seat on the couch that Janelle had set up for her next to the window. She knew the drill, but that didn't make her any more comfortable. She had secretly dubbed these sessions the "Witch Hunt Trials." It definitely always felt more like an inquisition than a therapy session, but even so, she settled in and faced Janelle, keeping her face expressionless.

"Are you ready?"

Janelle's question was unnecessary, and Jordan decided not to dignify it with a response.

"All right then," Janelle said after allowing the silence to linger for a few seconds. "We're going to start with a little bit of a discussion. Can you tell me what it is that you liked about your time with Taylor?"

The burning desire to keep their friendship, their connection, from anyone else was overruled by her need to survive this ordeal. She had snuck into Janelle's office and read through some of the books on her therapy options. It was best if she walked the line to avoid some of the archaic and frightening methods in there.

"She's fun," Jordan said slowly. "In fact, hanging out with her was probably the most fun I've had in years. She's funny, and we always laugh a lot. She taught me a lot about different things—everything from what friendship means to new types of music. More than anything, though, I trusted her in a way that I haven't trusted many friends. She is a good friend—the best friend I've ever had."

Janelle nodded her head, but the disgust she felt was evidenced by her sour expression.

When Jordan leaned back against the couch, she braced herself for whatever garbage would come out of Janelle's mouth.

"It was all a lie," Janelle said matter-of-factly. "It was all a game. She was attracted to you. She wanted to sleep with you and draw you into her world of sin. Of course she was fun. She is wild. She always has been. There's a certain allure to that kind of behavior. It's the same thing that has perpetuated all kinds of wrong and evil behavior throughout the centuries. It's the appeal of doing something scandalous. That's all she was—a fun and unique taste of something forbidden. And, of course, she let you think that you could trust her. She's got that charm. But, what did she do the minute you did? She enticed you to sin with her. Does that sound like a good friend?"

Jordan looked away, forcing her anger to find another target so she didn't lash out in frustration. Despite Janelle's best attempts, Jordan just could not hate Taylor, and she most certainly did not believe a single word out of Janelle's mouth about Taylor's ill intent. What they had wasn't fake. It couldn't have been.

She took a deep, steadying breath, before answering. "I don't know," she finally said, accepting the fact that arguing would only perpetuate the process even further.

"Well, I will explain it in a little better detail, then," Janelle said slowly, as if she were talking to a child. "When someone has homosexual desires, they are aligning themselves with things that are impure. They are inflicted with a demonic presence that feeds the lust and impure passions. Oftentimes that manifests itself in carrying out those desires with physical actions. Taylor has been involved in this type of thing before. You had not prior to your relationship with Ms. Reeves. Yet, she desired you. She befriended you, fully knowing how she felt about you. When you were weak and depressed, she took advantage of you."

Each word was like a blow to her stomach, and Jordan couldn't listen to anymore. It all sounded so clinical, so foreign, and so far from reality. Focusing on a piece of art hanging in the far corner of the room, she tried to drown out Janelle's voice.

Had it been true that her friendship had meant nothing to Taylor? Had Taylor only wanted to sleep with her? Was that all their time together had been about?

She hated herself for considering the questions, but even though she tried to convince herself that Janelle was just an angry, bitter woman, the remnants of doubt still hung in her head, clouding her reality. For days, all she had heard was that Taylor was the scum of the earth and that she had not cared for Jordan at all.

"She drew you in with her friendship, and then when she knew you were vulnerable, she struck, like a viper. With the age difference between the two of you, she really should be accused of robbing the cradle a little bit, in addition to everything else."

"We're both of age," Jordan retorted indignantly. "A few years between adults is not a big deal."

Janelle shook her head angrily, before running her fingers through her hair, messing it up and looking every bit like a parent trying to explain something to a stubborn toddler. The movement caused Jordan's blood to boil. She was sick of the condescension and the continual barrage of judgment. Janelle's brown eyes narrowed, and she cleared her throat.

"It is when the older one is drawing the younger one down a path of destruction. Her stupidity and her hormones forced her to try to ruin your life with this. This is not the type of situation you ever needed to be in, but she did not care. She is old enough to know better. You were playing with fire for the first time. She used proven tactics to charm you and entice you, and she should be held accountable for those despicable actions. She is despicable."

Jordan had been biting her tongue so hard that she tasted the sharp metallic taste of blood.

"Stop," she said, unable to hold it in any longer. "Just stop. I made these choices. I'm not a victim, and maybe we should consider the fact that I wanted these things to happen. Taylor didn't force me into anything. If anything, I moved the situation forward. I asked for this experience. I prodded Taylor along, even when she was hesitant. I wanted her, I desired her, and I asked for this to happen."

"Are you saying you're a lesbian?" The challenge in Janelle's voice was as plain as day.

"I'm not sure how to answer that."

"It's a yes or no question, Jordan," Janelle said condescendingly. "There is not really much to consider. Either you are or you aren't. I suppose it's a lot like being pregnant. There isn't a gray area. It's yes or no. However, we are going to cure you, either way."

"I don't know," Jordan said with a frustrated sigh. "I have a million things going through my head, and this barrage of questions every damn day isn't really helping me sort through them. Neither is the weird hypnosis thing you tried, or the negative associations. None of it is helping. You can't make me hate her," Jordan continued against her better judgment. "I just don't, and I won't. It's that simple. This process is doing nothing but damage. I don't know how to answer some of these questions, and each time I try to think something over, you jump on it like I've just admitted to being an accessory to a crime. I just need time and a little bit of quiet so that I can sort through this on my own."

"You mean you want to sort through it with Taylor."

The assumption got under Jordan's skin, and she raised her voice. "No, I mean I want to sort through it on my own. Sure, this started with Taylor, but this is a thought process about my own identity. It's something I need to figure out on my own."

"Are you saying you don't need Taylor? Because I think you feel like you do."

"I am self-reliant and independent," Jordan said pointedly. "I am strong. I don't need Taylor. I don't really need anyone. Did I want and love Taylor? Yes, of course I did. I loved her in a way that made me question things about myself, about the world around me, and about everything I've ever known to be true. I wanted her in a way that made me ache inside, and yes, I still do. Maybe I always will have that yearning. Maybe I won't. Maybe it's a phase, as I've been told. Maybe it was a mistake. But if so, it was the most beautiful mistake I've ever made, and I owe it to the both of us to figure out what is going on inside of my head and my heart. And, I can't do that under your constant scrutiny."

The confession spilled out far too easily, and Jordan realized she had reached her breaking point. It was as if an epiphany sprung up from nowhere, and she knew that she couldn't stay here any longer.

Janelle was seething in anger. There was no way for her to hide it now, and when she spoke, her voice shook.

"You still have a week left of this so-called scrutiny, and I won't have you speaking of loving her during this time. If you remember, that's one of the first rules of this therapy. You have to submit to accepting that you don't love her. It wasn't love. It was lust—gross, misguided lust."

Jordan could not and would not agree anymore. She had gone along with Janelle's games, pretending that she agreed and wanting a way out of these feelings for Taylor. She had listened to enough of the bullshit.

"Stop telling me what you think I did or did not feel," she said, standing up from the couch. "You have no idea. You weren't there. You didn't live it. I did."

She knew she should stop, but she couldn't contain the desire to put Janelle in her place. "It wasn't gross or misguided. The only thing gross and misguided in this room is the way you are degrading everyone. I'm still trying to reconcile what I feel with what I've been taught. I'm still trying to come to terms with what I've done, and determine whether or not I'm gay—or if that's something I can get past. I don't want to be gay. You know that, and I know that. But, I won't sit here any longer and listen to you degrade what I feel in such a manner."

"Sit back down," Janelle instructed.

Jordan shook her head defiantly. "I've had enough."

Anger flashed in Janelle's eyes. "If you walk out of this house before your sessions are up, I'll tell your parents."

"Tell them," Jordan said with a shrug. "Actually, you know what? I'm tired of fighting along your rules. I will tell them. I'll tell them tomorrow morning."

"Stop," Janelle bellowed. "I can help you. Just let me help you."

"You're not helping me. I'm not your project, and this little thing you've got set up isn't going to work. You haven't been able to change what I feel yet, and you're not ever going to be able to. You're not a magician. You're a misguided counselor with a superhero complex, and I'm over it. I'm over this whole thing."

She spun on her heel and headed for the door, but Janelle rushed to her and grabbed her arm before she could get to the door handle.

"Please get your hands off me," Jordan said, feeling the anger brewing within her.

"Don't give up on fighting this," Janelle said, gripping tightly. "I know it's hard, but if you give in, your life as you know it is over. Do you really think your parents are going to be understanding? You may think they're going to love you regardless, but you'll be wrong. How many small-town families do you know that would be overjoyed to find out that their daughter is a filthy, sinful lesbian?"

Each word hit like a strike to the cheek, stopping Jordan in her tracks. Janelle was echoing the thoughts that had kept Jordan up each night. Her family wouldn't understand. They wouldn't be forgiving and loving, and if she thought she had a problem making friends before, it would be even worse if everyone knew.

Janelle loosened the grip on Jordan's arm, but Jordan made no attempt at escape.

"Your mistakes won't change what's right and wrong," Janelle said. "It won't change their minds, and it will definitely change your relationship with them. Is that what you want?"

Jordan couldn't muster a response. There was enough self-loathing flowing through her body without Janelle's help, but Janelle didn't seem to mind heaping on a little extra.

"Do you really want to disappoint them and make them question where they went wrong as parents?"

Refusing to cry anymore, Jordan gulped back the knot in her throat and quietly took her seat back beside Janelle on the couch.

As she pulled her feet under her knees to sit on the couch like a child, she thought she could hear the small part of her independence crying as it took its final breath. She knew that this defeat wasn't permanent, but it didn't help calm the storm within her soul.

"Good girl," Janelle commented, sending another shot of fresh anger through Jordan's entire being.

Forcing deep breaths, she closed her eyes so that she didn't snap again. She needed to focus on survival—not physical, but spiritual. She needed to try to retain some shred of who she was throughout this entire demeaning and degrading process. If she could manage that, she would have victory. Then, she could have the opportunity to sort through all of the chaos in her head on her own.

She raised her head and looked Janelle in the eye, mentally preparing for whatever barbs she might throw.

Instead of more harsh words, Janelle offered an unreadable expression before reaching into her notebook.

"Memorize these scriptures, so that you can recite them any time the temptation strikes," she said, handing Jordan a few note cards. "When you've got that done, come find me in the kitchen."

With that, Janelle stood and exited the room. Jordan stared blankly at the cards, feeling the numbness surround her.

One by one, she read the cards, trying to commit them to memory, but she was fairly certain that even these words that she had always believed would never be enough to ever get the searing memory of Taylor's touch out of her head.

Still, she memorized the verses, said a silent prayer and left the room after taking a few minutes to herself. It was best if she got this over with as soon as possible.

Walking to the kitchen, she set the cards on the table and began reciting the verses to Janelle, even though her back was turned.

When Jordan finished, Janelle turned around slowly. "Very good," she commented, showing as little amusement as possible. "Keep those note cards and pull them out whenever you're tempted to even contact the one who coerced you into this world of sin."

Jordan had to stifle a laugh. "You mean Taylor?"

Janelle stiffened at the mention of her name. "Yes. I've been thinking that this will probably be more productive if we stop actually using her name. You need to disassociate with the girl you thought you knew and begin to see her for what she truly is. From this point forward, she will not be referred to as Taylor during the therapy process."

Deciding not to fight her on the ridiculous mandate, Jordan walked out of the room and shut the door to her temporary bedroom.

Once in the safety of her own privacy, she took a few calming breaths and closed her eyes for some meditation. It was time to battle with her own demons, with the ghosts of what she was—what she had always been. More than anything, it was time to find a little self-acceptance.

CHAPTER FIFTEEN

A weekend away from the judgment had been just what Taylor needed, but it hadn't been near long enough. As she pulled her truck back into town, she wished she had made the decision to stay.

"Running away is never the answer," she reminded herself aloud.

After surrounding herself with friends and gaining some insight, she knew it was time to face the truth. If she was ever going to be happy, she was going to have to finally take a stand for what she believed in. There would be no more shame, no more hiding, and no more secrets.

At almost thirty years old, there was no sense in the lies. It was time, and she had spent the entire drive home building the courage to shine some light onto the current situation and onto her past. She was tired of fighting against what she believed, just as she was tired of those like Jordan getting hurt in the process.

As she pulled into her driveway, her phone vibrated with an incoming text message.

She picked it up and read Amy's encouraging words.

You have a family here, and we have always loved you. We will be here for you if you need anything. Good luck!

She smiled at the encouragement. Of course her friends in Oklahoma would be there for her. They always had been. They had always known about her love life, and she never kept any secrets from them. Her parents, though, would undoubtedly be a different story. Nonetheless, it was time to take care of what she should have taken care of years ago.

Looking at her reflection in the rearview mirror, she saw in her eyes the epitome of freedom. The fear was gone, as was the doubt and uncertainty.

Instead, she was face-to-face with the new Taylor—a girl whose bravery and self-respect outweighed anything bad that may come from the rest of the day.

In her head, she replayed her plan over and over again before finally making herself leave the truck to put away her luggage. She did so quickly, suddenly not wanting to delay even a minute longer than necessary.

Never before had she felt so determined. This plan was for her, but if it did something to ease Jordan's burden as well, it would be even better.

Over the course of the weekend, she had come to the realization that even though she was a grown woman, Jordan was still impressionable. There was no doubt in Taylor's mind that her own refusal to come out and be who she was had influenced Jordan's own self-doubt and self-loathing. She wanted to be true to herself, and in the process, she wanted to show Jordan there was no shame in what had happened or in who she was.

With one last glance in the mirror, Taylor left the house, sure only that her life was never going to be the same again.

On the drive over, she cranked up the sound to the latest pride anthem "Brave" by Sara Bareilles and soaked in the words. Sara was right. It was far past time to be brave. She smiled, taking in deep breaths and keeping her focus. She had lived in the shadows for too long, and she was ready to shine light onto the pride that she felt for her truest identity.

Once at her parents' house, she fought the urge to knock. This was just an ordinary day, and there was no need to treat it with more formality than it deserved.

She walked up the front steps and opened the door, a chaotic storm of uncertainty suddenly flooding through her in place of the determination that had existed only seconds before.

"This is why people take care of this in their teens," she muttered to herself as she shut the door behind her.

"Mom, Dad, are you home?" she called throughout the house.

Flitting around like a fairy, her mother danced through the entryway. "Taylor!" she exclaimed excitedly, as if it had been weeks or months—not merely a few days—since she had seen her daughter. "How was your trip? Did you have a good time? Did you tell Amy hi for me?"

The questions flurried out, sending Taylor's nerves once again on a roller coaster. Her mother was always so excitable and full of energy, and Taylor wished she would just calm down for a few minutes. Her announcement would, no doubt, do the trick.

"The trip was good," Taylor said slowly. "I had a good time, and I made some important decisions."

Her mother's eyebrows shot up immediately, asking the million questions that she didn't speak for once.

"Is Dad home?" Taylor asked, moving past her mother into the kitchen.

"He's in the garage working on his old Mustang," she said with a laugh. "Men and their toys. You know, someday you're going to have a husband with a million little hobbies too, and it'll drive you crazy."

The endless blabber was nothing new; nor was the mention of Taylor's future husband. She fought the feelings of stress rising in her bloodstream and instead poured herself a glass of water.

"I'd like to make dinner for the two of you tonight, if that's okay," Taylor said, trying to keep her tone even.

"Oh, that sounds wonderful, sweetie," her mother gushed. "What did you have in mind?"

"I thought I would grill us some steaks and make potatoes."

"You're so sweet. That would be perfect."

"Great," Taylor said, not feeling the sentiment at all. "I'll go get started then. I've got the stuff in the car."

She quickly went out to her car and gathered the items she had pulled from her own freezer and pantry. There was no sense in making it awkward. Instead, she wanted things to seem as normal as possible. She would cook them dinner, as she often did, and then she would tell them during dinner. Besides, the extra preparation time for the food would give her a few more minutes to prepare herself emotionally.

She didn't want to cry. She had already decided that much. This was not something of which she was ashamed or afraid; instead, it was an integral part of her happiness. She didn't want them to think otherwise.

Even though her hands were shaking and her thoughts were going a million miles an hour, she managed to grill the steaks to perfection. And as she sat in the kitchen with her mother waiting for the potatoes to finish in the oven, she let herself get lost in the normalcy of an afternoon discussion.

They covered everything from the way the rose bushes out back were holding up under recent rains to the family that couldn't pay their bills and came to the church for help. Within a matter of minutes, Taylor was caught up on everything she had missed in this tiny town over the weekend.

As she pulled the potatoes out of the oven, she wished that type of normalcy would still hang over them after she made her announcement, but she knew that it wouldn't. She was about to change all of their lives permanently.

"Dad," Taylor called, poking her head out the garage door. "Dinner is ready."

He looked up, equally surprised and happy to see her. She soaked it in, knowing that look would come significantly less often in the coming days—maybe even weeks. That was if she even saw them. Knowing that her stint at the church would probably come to a crashing halt, she had decided that she would take a leave of absence anyway and would quietly step back. That way, if they didn't want to see her or deal with the mistakes of their daughter, they didn't have to. It would be less painful for them both.

He joined them in the kitchen and said grace to bless the meal before they all took their respective places at the table. "This looks wonderful," her dad commented, spearing a bite of steak and popping it into his mouth. He gave her a smile of appreciation when he swallowed. "Tastes wonderful, too," he commented. "How was your trip? We didn't expect you by this evening, but this is a nice surprise."

"I decided to come see you and thank you for everything," she said. "You both are so good to me, and I wanted to show you that I appreciate that."

Her father accepted it at face value, but her mother's expression showed concern. "Thank you," she said hesitantly. "Is there something wrong, Taylor?"

Taylor quickly shook her head to dismiss her mother's fears and took a bite of her steak. After enjoying the bite, she pushed her plate back slightly.

"Nothing is wrong," she said. "But I do have some things I want to talk to the two of you about."

"Is this what you mentioned earlier?" her mother asked. "About the things you figured out on your trip?"

Taylor nodded, trying to gauge both of their moods, before deciding that it probably didn't matter anyway. They could both be in the best of moods, and she was still going to turn their worlds upside down. She took a deep breath and proceeded.

"I realized that I need to be more honest about a few things in my life," she said, choosing her words carefully. "You know that growing up as preacher's kids, the boys and I often felt the need to hide things from you. We had this preconceived notion that we needed to try to be perfect. We were always in the spotlight—always in the front pew at church—always the token example of how kids are supposed to behave. We learned quickly to adapt, to hide, to fight for survival the only way kids know how—by lying. It carried over to when we were teenagers, hiding the fact that we tried alcohol or that we smoked. I know you all saw through most of those half-truths, but some of those habits we learned early carried over with me to adulthood."

The look of devastation on her mother's face was almost enough to make her stop, but she had to continue. She had gotten this far, and the fact that her mother was disappointed in not knowing everything in her daughter's life was the fuel that she needed to keep going. If she wanted to know everything, she was going to very shortly.

"Are you in some kind of trouble?" her father asked, breaking the silence.

"No," Taylor said. "This is kind of hard for me to put into words, so please have patience. Bear with me." She took a drink of water to steady her thoughts.

"I told you that we resorted to hiding things from you as kids. We all did it. Only, I didn't stop when I was a kid. Instead, when I hit about eighteen, I made a difficult discovery—one that forever changed my life. It is something that has shaped every thought of every day since, and something that I have actively hidden from you out of fear. I'm not quite sure what that fear was, but I knew that if you knew, it would change things for us, and I wasn't ready for that."

The further she went on, the more her mother's eyes widened. Her father remained calm and steady, as if bracing for a coming storm.

"I can't hide anymore. I can't deny who I am or what I do in my life. It's not worth it to keep a part of myself hidden for anyone's comfort—even for my own comfort. It's time for me to tell you something, but I don't want you to make rash comments, please. Hear me out."

She turned her attention to her mother. "Mom, do you remember how when I was younger, we would stay up late and pray for my future husband?"

Her mother nodded and smiled at the memory, despite the turmoil in her eyes.

"You always told me you wanted me to find someone who made me come alive, who cherished me, reminded me that I was beautiful, never took advantage, was patient and kind, inspired me, taught me new things about the world, and loved me deeply.

"Dad, you always said that one day you hoped I found someone who delighted in the way my eyes light up when I smile, someone who noticed all of the little things, who helped me, who reminded me to dream and to chase my passions, who made every day special for me. Do you both remember that?"

They both nodded, her dad suddenly looking expectant and hopeful.

"Do you still want that for me?" she asked.

"More than anything," her mother said with a smile. "That's still my prayer every night. I want my little girl to find the happiness and security of love."

Her father nodded his assurance, but the hesitation was clear in his eyes.

"Good, because I've found that someone," Taylor said, using her love for Jordan as the strength she needed to continue. "I've found all that and so much more—in the most amazing and curious person, in a person you would least expect. I have found someone who makes me feel as if I've spent the rest of my life asleep before we met. I found the one who challenges me—and even frustrates me at times—but makes me grow as a person. The only problem is, I am pretty sure that the two of you won't approve."

"Oh darling, if you're happy, we're happy," her mother said quickly. "I just don't know why you've kept it from us."

"We'd like to meet him," her father added. "I'm sure your mother is right, but I'd like to give him my stamp of approval."

She raised her hands to stop them both.

"It's not a him. It's a her."

She took one last deep breath, let her words sink in, and blurted it out.

"I'm gay," she said. "I'm a lesbian."

In the seconds that followed, she tried to catch her breath. A part of her felt free, but the other part wished she could snatch the words out of the air and take the horrified expression off her mother's face with them.

Her mother looked like she wanted to run but her legs were too weak, as if she had just found out her child was terminally ill.

Her father stood up at the head of the table, no longer interested in the food that still sat on his plate.

"What did we do wrong?" he asked quietly to himself.

"Dad, it's not like that. It's not a disease. It's not a result of your parenting. It's just who I am."

He shook his head, refusing to believe it.

"We'll get you help," he said quickly. "I know of some places that offer therapy. We'll help you through this. It doesn't have to be like this."

"No."

Taylor's refusal was simple but stern, drawing a questioning look from her father.

"I won't get therapy. I won't try to change this about myself. I spent years loathing myself for it, unable to tell anyone. I spent countless nights crying myself to sleep and wishing it could all be different. I even spent a few years trying to convince myself that I could be happy some other way, and denying my happiness made me a better person. It didn't. It made me depressed and suicidal, and I won't go back to that place. I'm proud of who I am, and I hope you can still love me—just as I am."

"Of course we love you," her father said evenly. "But that doesn't mean we condone this nonsense."

"Who is she?" her mother finally spoke.

"Someone who would prefer that I don't disclose that information, I'm sure," Taylor said. "But that's not important."

"Yes, it is. I need to know who talked you into this and who made you think that this was a good idea."

"Mom," Taylor said incredulously. "She didn't do this to me. This is just who I am."

"I think you should go for now," her father interjected. "Will I see you tomorrow?"

"You still want me at the church?" she asked in shock.

"I think that's the best place for you," he said. "I'll have a therapist there first thing in the morning to get started helping you."

She shook her head again. He was clearly and blatantly ignoring everything she had said.

"I'm going to take some time off," she said. "You can get rid of my position if you'd like or you can fill it. You can hold it for me if you'd like, but I think I'm going to give you both some time to process everything. Until you agree not to try to change me, I'm not coming back to that church. It's that important to me."

He nodded, making a hard line out of his lips. No one ever stood up to him in that manner, and it was clear that he wasn't sure how to handle the situation.

"I love you both," she said as she made her way to the door.

With one last glance at the table, she couldn't help but see two parents who thought they had lost their only daughter.

In her heart, she felt the same sorrow they did. Not only had they lost a daughter, but she had lost her job and her parents in one afternoon.

Once in her truck, she forced a deep breath. Despite all the heartache of family dysfunction, she was going to chalk the day up as a win. She was free to be herself. For the first time in her life, she was free to live.

More than anything, she wanted to call Jordan and have her come celebrate the occasion with her, but she resisted the urge.

This was a personal freedom—and a challenge she had conquered for herself. She needed to celebrate this on her own.

As she drove away from their house, she couldn't help but feel like maybe this was what it felt like to grow up. Taking the long way home, she circled by Janelle's house, only to see Jordan's car parked out front.

She longed to go to the girl and tell her there was another way, aside from all the hiding and secrets, but she knew that Jordan was going to have to figure out those things on her own. She recounted all the times that she had been told to just come out.

"It will make things so much better."

"It'll be easy."

All the reassuring words from her friends played through her mind, and some of them had been right, while others hadn't been. The truth was that it was different for everyone, and maybe everyone had to come to their own peace in their own time to deal with it properly.

She sighed and tried to refocus on the road ahead, but movement in the upstairs window of Janelle's house caught the corner of her eye. Looking up briefly, she saw Jordan's face fill the window.

It was heartbreaking, as if she were the maiden locked away in the tower, waiting on someone to rescue her. Taylor waved and smiled in Jordan's direction. It was too far away for Taylor to really make out Jordan's expression, so she continued to drive. If Jordan wanted to talk, she would find a way to call or text. If not, Taylor would respect her space.

Turning down a side street, she quickly exited the neighborhood. The last thing she needed was for someone to turn her in for stalking or something similar, and she knew that Janelle was not above doing something like that.

It would be best to keep her distance—for both her sake and for Jordan's. As she drove away, she couldn't get the image of those haunted green eyes out of her head. Whatever was happening in that house, she wished Jordan didn't have to be a part of it.

But, maybe someday, she could find freedom as well.

CHAPTER SIXTEEN

For a minute, it felt as if all oxygen escaped the room and Jordan's thoughts went into a blur. Seeing Taylor drive by had undone her in an inexplicable way, and she fought her warring emotions. She wasn't sure if she wanted to run after Taylor and throw caution to the wind, or run screaming in the other direction.

After all, Taylor had been down this road before. She had known exactly what she was getting Jordan into, and Jordan couldn't help but feel a little resentful. Somehow, Jordan had ended up here in anti-gay therapy, and Taylor was free to live her life as she pleased.

In the back of her mind she knew she wasn't being fair to Taylor and she was being unreasonable, but it didn't stop her emotions.

"Loneliness brings out the worst in people."

Her mother's words echoed in her mind. Every time someone acted poorly or lashed out in anger, those were usually the words her mother chose to mark the situation. It was as if every time there was a cranky old man, her mother assumed he was alone. Whether or not she was right most of the time, she certainly would have been right now.

As she sat alone in this dreadful room, Jordan's mind had raced to every possibility from screaming at Taylor to giving Janelle a taste of her own blackmail. She truly was the worst version of herself that she had ever seen.

With a sigh, she closed her eyes and attempted to bring back some of her inner peace—even a shred of her self-worth.

After a moment of failed meditation, she knew there was only one logical thing to do. Before she went crazy, she had to get out of this house.

With it being the weekend, Janelle was home, which was problematic. There was no way she was going to let Jordan out of her sight without a valid excuse.

More than anything, she wanted to just go sit in the park, write in her journal, and feel like a normal human being, instead of the test rat that she felt like most days. But, that would never be allowed.

When she had formulated a plan, she changed clothes, straightened her makeup and headed downstairs.

"Janelle," she called out from the hallway, feeling like an escapee who was unsure of where her captor might be waiting for her.

"In the kitchen," she answered.

Jordan rounded the corner. "I'm thinking of going to spend the day with my mom," she said, knowing both that the excuse would be checked and that it would work. "I haven't seen her in a while, and she and I need a little bit of time to catch up. I think it would do us both some good."

"Okay," Janelle agreed all too easily.

There was no doubt in Jordan's mind that the minute she walked out the door, Janelle would call to see what her mom was doing this afternoon. Quickly, she sent her mom a text telling her that she was coming over for a visit. It was best to avoid confrontation in this volatile situation.

"See you later," Jordan said as she turned on her heel to go.

"Stay away from Taylor," Janelle reminded.

"Will do," Jordan said dryly.

On the drive over, she rejoiced in the simple freedoms of life. It seemed like she was trapped in a twelve-year-old's world these days, void of all of the freedoms that she had as a normal twenty-something.

Turning up the radio as loud as it would go, she let herself get lost in the music. It was a welcome escape from drowning in her thoughts as she had been doing so often lately.

Once her vehicle sat in her parents' driveway, she wasn't sure this had been such a good idea. Her mom was like a detective, always able to sniff out when something was the least bit wrong in Jordan's life. There was no doubt she would have a slew of questions for Jordan. She tried to brace herself for that and to prepare herself to keep her emotions at bay. The last thing she needed was to break down in front of her mother, who would undoubtedly relay the information back to Janelle.

Then, they'd have to start all over at square one. It was best if everyone just thought things were going fine in Jordan's world. It would be much easier that way.

Forcing a smile onto her face, she got out of her car.

"There's my girl!"

The smile on her mother's face as she bounded down the driveway like a happy four-year-old turned Jordan's smile into a genuine expression. It was nice to feel welcome, and nothing quite beat the feeling of coming home where love flowed freely.

She ignored the little nagging voice in her head that asked how long that love would flow. Instead, she focused her attention on the woman in front of her, beaming with pride.

"You look good, Mom," she commented. "Those workouts are paying off."

It was an easy compliment as she took in the sight of her mother, toned and trim. Aside from being a few inches taller, she was practically a replica of her mother. She looked her up and down, noting the same green eyes, delicate facial structure, and dimpled smile. "I hope I look half as good as you one of these days," she added with a smile.

"Thanks," her mom said with a slight shrug. "It was time for me to get in shape. But don't give me this half as good stuff. You're beautiful."

"Well, you're the envy of all the women on the block, I'm sure," she said, pulling her mother in for a hug and brushing off the compliment. She felt anything but beautiful these days. She felt like a mess. "How have you been?"

"I've been good—but your father and I have both been worried about you. I was so excited when you said you were coming over to visit. I know it's only been a week or so, but I feel like I never see you anymore."

"I know," Jordan said apologetically. "Life has been pretty busy lately."

Her mother finally let go of the hug and backed away, looking at her daughter from head to toe. "I can't wait to hear all about it," she said. "Let's go inside. I just made some fresh lemonade."

Jordan followed behind her, enjoying the normalcy and comfort of the moment. She wasn't a science experiment today. She was just a girl, having an afternoon with her mother. She desperately wished there was a way to convey her gratitude to her mother for this moment, but she knew that doing so would only open up a floodgate of questions she wasn't prepared to deal with quite yet.

The brisk air from the air-conditioner working overtime hit Jordan as she entered the front door. "It's been so hot outside," her mother explained knowingly. "Your father likes to keep it cool, and you know how that goes. We play by his rules because it's easier."

Jordan laughed. That had been their joke her entire life. It was always easier to give in to her father than to fight him at every turn. As her mom poured a glass of lemonade for them both, Jordan wondered if that was where she had first learned to just go with the flow and not make situations more difficult than they needed to be.

If it hadn't been for her lifetime of diehard allegiance to her mother, she was sure she might have caught on earlier that there were things that were definitely worth fighting for. Instead, she had accepted that some people's opinions couldn't be changed and that at times, it was best to simply stay silent.

It unnerved her how clearly she suddenly saw her current situation. Once again, she was choosing not to disclose truths to protect the comfort of her mother and father—a tactic she had witnessed numerous times throughout her childhood.

She took a drink of the lemonade after her mom sat it in front of her and took a seat across from her at the kitchen table.

"What's been going on?"

The question from her mother was a simple one, but Jordan didn't know how to answer it. For the first time, there was nothing in her life that she felt she could share with her mother—her oldest friend.

She shrugged. "Now that you ask, I'm not quite sure," she said, masking her uncertainty with a laugh. "There's nothing in particular that's different, but life just seems to be moving at a faster pace, keeping me busier than usual." She watched as the eyes across the table narrowed.

"I don't buy it," her mother said, using the detective skills that had been finely honed over her years of parenthood. "What's really going on? I can see it in your eyes that something is amiss."

When Jordan didn't offer any sort of explanation, her mother pressed. "You can talk to me," she urged. "You know I'm always here for you."

"I know, Mom," Jordan said. "Thank you for that. To be honest, I'm not quite sure I even know what's going on these days."

Her mom reached across the table and grabbed her hand. "Is everything okay, sweetheart? Should I be worried?"

Jordan shook her head. She wished she could nod and tell her mother everything. Then, if things were different, she would at least have an ally. As it was, she knew that wouldn't happen. Instead, she sadly shook away the possibility that anything was wrong.

"I think it's just mainly a life adjustment," Jordan said, deciding she could draw the similarities between her current situation and her transition to not playing basketball. "Things are changing, and I'm working to find myself in the shuffle. I'm growing up, and I just have a lot to sort out, I think."

"Do you want to talk about it?"

"I think I'm going to have to accept the changes myself before I can expect other people to accept them. I'm just not quite there, and I'm not sure if I ever will be."

"You don't need anyone else's approval. Find out what you need to find out, and then just be happy. Be you, and be happy, Jordan. That's all that matters. You are a smart, talented and beautiful girl who has the world at your fingertips. Your father and I are proud of you, and we love you. We'll always be in your corner."

Jordan felt her eyes well up with tears. She had always been certain of that sentiment until recently. Now she wasn't so sure that unconditional love truly came without condition. They might promise to always be in her corner, but that could change in a matter of minutes. She could be the one to change it.

Moving over to the side of the table, her mom scooped her into a hug.

"It's going to be okay."

She tried to assure her, but it only made the tears fall more quickly down Jordan's face. It wasn't okay, and it might not ever be again. Her world as she knew it had crumbled.

"Talk to me, please."

The request was simple, and she didn't know how to turn it down. Turning her face upward to make eye contact with her mother, she felt fresh fear enter her body.

"I don't really even know how to explain it all," she said.

"Just try."

Jordan took a deep breath, preparing herself for somewhat of a partial disclosure.

"Things are just so messed up right now. My world feels like it's upside down. I'm second-guessing everything I've ever known or believed in. Things are just a disaster."

"A beautiful disaster," her mother commented and nodded knowingly. "It sounds a lot like growing up to me."

"I guess so," Jordan said, wishing it were that simple a concept.

"What's got you so confused?"

Jordan gulped. Confused was exactly the word she had hoped to avoid. She shook her head, casting her eyes downward as she tried to gather her thoughts.

"I'm just going through a hard time, I think."

In the moments of silence that followed, her mother's brow creased as she searched for the right words to comfort her obviously distraught daughter. "Have you talked to Janelle about any of it, sweetie?" she finally asked.

"Unfortunately," Jordan said, regretting the word as soon as it was out of her mouth.

"Why is that unfortunate?"

The genuine concern in her mother's voice made Jordan wish she had just kept her mouth shut about all of it. "It's not," she said quickly. "It's just that Janelle is reading too much into everything I tell her, and she's been really judgmental and weird about things. She has rules I have to follow and just gets strange about every situation."

In an instant, Jordan watched as Janelle became someone who was harming Jordan instead of a lifelong friend in her mother's mind.

"Are your therapy sessions hurting more than they're helping? Do you need to stop seeing her? If she is hurting you, I'll take care of it."

While Jordan appreciated the "mama bear" reaction, she wanted to just leave Janelle out of this conversation completely.

"It's fine, Mom, but thank you. I'll handle it all."

Squeezing her knee, her mother gave Jordan a smile. "You don't have to handle it on your own. Why don't you try to talk to me about it, and then maybe you won't need to talk to Janelle."

Jordan sighed. She had opened up the can of worms, and now she had to give her mother something, or she was going to get upset.

Just as she had done when Jordan was a small child, her mother leaned over and kissed her on the head, cupping her face between her hands. "I love you," she said gently, bringing back memories of the hundreds of times she had done exactly that over the years.

Nostalgia washed over Jordan, making her long for simpler times. But, the questioning look in her mother's eyes brought her back to reality. In this moment, nothing was simple.

"I got myself into a bit of a bad situation," she finally admitted. "I think I made a mistake, but I'm not sure. It doesn't feel like a mistake, but I'm facing the consequences either way."

Jordan looked down, and then regained eye contact with her mother, who looked even more confused after Jordan's vague and jumbled confession.

"Talk to me, Jordan," she urged. "Whatever it is, I can take it. Stop dancing around the truth, and just talk to me. I'm here for you."

Her words all started to run together in Jordan's mind, drowned out by the reminders in her head that her mother's view of her could be forever altered by a simple confession. Finally deciding to bite the bullet, she felt—more than participated in—the blurting out of the truth she never wanted her mother to know.

"I kissed Taylor...or Taylor kissed me. I'm not really sure."

She watched closely for a reaction, but her mother masked it well.

Leaning in more closely as if she was gaining top-secret information, her mother tilted her head to the side. "Do you like girls?"

"No," Jordan's response was quick.

"Do you like boys?"

"Yes."

"Okay, do you like Taylor?"

The sheer insight in the question took the air out of Jordan's lungs. She had been trying to answer the same question all along, even though she knew the answer all too well. But, now the question hung in the air so blatantly calling out to her to answer.

Instead, she looked away. "I don't know," she finally answered.

In the awkward silence that followed, Jordan wished she could run away and do this all over again. She should have never come here, and she definitely should have never trusted herself to keep her secret.

Her mother cleared her throat, forcing Jordan to stop plotting the quickest escape route. "I love you—no matter what," she said gently. "You know that, right?"

Jordan nodded. She had honestly been unsure of the answer until just now, but the words were reassuring.

"But, I'm not going to tell your father about this," she continued. "You and I both know how he would react. So, if you need to talk, I'm not sure I'm equipped to deal with this in a proper manner, but I will be here for you. You're my daughter, and I'll help you through whatever you need."

Even though unconditional love was being expressed, Jordan could hear the unspoken undertones. The message was clear: her father wouldn't approve, and if she needed help to fix this or make it go away, her mother was more than willing to help.

She had never doubted that her parents wouldn't approve, and now she had solid evidence to back up that theory. Now, the only question that hung over her head was whether or not she wanted to make it go away.

After assuring her mom that there was nothing to figure out, and that she was just being an overdramatic girl, she left the house feeling empty.

There was no denying the fact that she was alone in this battle, any more than there was no denying that she was more confused than ever.

On the drive back to Janelle's house, she tried to waste as much time as possible. She didn't want to be back under lock and key. Instead, she longed for some basic freedoms, but she apparently had forgone that option the minute she had started sleeping with Taylor.

"Be strong enough to stand alone, smart enough to know when you need help, and brave enough to ask for it."

She repeated the words over and over again, reminding herself of one of her lifelong mottos. If need be, she was strong enough to stand alone. That much she had already proven. But she also knew that it might be time for help—legitimate and beneficial help.

Deciding to go on a moment's courage, she picked up her phone and dialed the number that she had memorized, despite the urgings she had received to just forget it and all details of Taylor Reeves.

After a few rings, she heard Taylor's confused voice fill the line.

"Hello?"

"Hey," Jordan said, her voice small and weak sounding.

"Are you okay?"

"I'd like to talk if you have some time this afternoon."

She waited in the silent seconds that followed, unsure if Taylor would even want to bother with all the drama that Jordan had caused.

"Sorry," Taylor said after a moment. "You just caught me by surprise. In fact, I wasn't even sure it was really you when you called. I thought maybe Janelle was playing some kind of game, warning me to stay away—or else. But, yeah, I'd love to chat whenever you're free."

Jordan felt relief flood through her. "Can I head to your house in a few minutes?"

Taylor's smile was evident in her voice. "Of course."

Jordan hung up and tried to ignore the way her body reacted at the thought of that beautiful smile. Fighting to regain control of her shivering body, she headed back, giving into the magnetism of her heart.

If nothing else, being with Taylor would give her the chance to talk through her fears, doubts and feelings—free from judgment. It was something she had needed more than anything else in the world. For all of the support she offered, her mother didn't understand, and she probably never would. This was not something she had ever dealt with; nor was it something she was comfortable addressing.

With Taylor, though, Jordan knew that she was free—free to talk and sort through the chaos without wondering if love would be removed with her words.

Once she arrived in front of Taylor's house, she couldn't get out of the car fast enough. Any hesitation that would have held her back had vanished. There was only one person she wanted to see, consequences be damned.

She reached up and knocked quickly and steadily on the door, waiting with growing anticipation. Before her fist could knock a second time, Taylor opened the door, her smile stretching across her face.

Without a word, Jordan threw her arms around Taylor, pulling her into an embrace. While she resisted the urge to take in Taylor's scent, she couldn't deny the way her body clung tighter than it should.

"I'm happy to see you too," Taylor said with a laugh, pulling her even closer before stepping back to take in the sight of Jordan.

"It feels like it's been forever," Jordan said. "I feel like I've been gone from you for so long."

"I know the feeling. Hours turned into days, and days into weeks, and before long it felt like you might not even know me if you saw me."

Jordan laughed, breaking the seriousness of the moment. "Look at us, acting like drama queens. At least we're here together now. I've missed my friend."

Jordan tried to ignore the way Taylor's smile dropped slightly at the use of the word "friend," but when she couldn't, she looked away momentarily.

"You said you wanted to talk?" Taylor asked, taking a seat on the couch. "Come sit with me."

Nodding nervously, Jordan took a seat on the opposite end of the couch, making sure to leave some distance between the two of them. If she knew anything at all, it was that her overpowering lust for Taylor couldn't be contained. She was going to have to stay on guard, or she would end up back in Taylor's arms—receiving as much of a mind fuck as a physical one. That was the last thing she needed, at least until she got her thoughts back in order.

"What's going on? How have you spent your weeks in solitary confinement?"

Jordan gazed at her, simply taking in the quirky way she chose to word her sentences and enjoying the comfort of her company. Shaking her head, she tried to explain what she had been through since she had last spoken with Taylor.

"In a word, it's been hell. I see no one, aside from Janelle and occasionally Trevor. Janelle is the bitch she's always been, and Trevor goes back and forth between being stoned out of his mind and mentally absent from what's happening in the world around him to hitting on me. I guess I'd do the same if I had her for a mother, though. She's awful. She's overbearing. She's condescending. I have these torturous therapy sessions in which she tries to make me hate you, and if I answer wrong, I receive strange assignments that feel more like punishments. She monitors everything I do, and if I step out of line, I face the fear of her running and telling my parents."

She took a deep breath. "I told my mom some of what happened, though."

Taylor's nose crinkled as her face cracked into a smile. "You told her? Good for you. Take some wind out of Janelle's sails. If she doesn't have the power of blackmail, she has nothing to hold you there."

"That's just the problem," Jordan said. "I couldn't tell her everything, and even though she tried to still show me love, it was difficult for her to take in what I told her. I just don't know if I can risk her finding out the full truth—or worse, my father finding out what I've been doing. They would both be crushed, and I'm still not sure that this lifestyle is even what I want. I just don't know what to do anymore."

Taylor nodded and tried to keep her facial expressions neutral as she listened.

"It's not that I don't want you," Jordan said, realizing how her words must have sounded. "I'm not trying to figure out if I want to be with you. Of course I do. But, it's just that my world feels like it's spinning, and I can't get it to stop. I can't tell what's right and wrong anymore, and I don't want to do something that's wrong."

"Does it feel wrong when we're together?"

"Nothing has ever felt more right than when I get so lost in you that I can't tell where I end and you begin."

Reaching out gently and slowly, as if Jordan were a timid animal who might run at the slightest movement, Taylor extended her hand. The invitation was clear, and it packed more power than Jordan would have liked to admit. Electricity coursed through her body as she closed the distance and grabbed Taylor's hand.

Sitting hand in hand on the couch with Taylor, Jordan felt her passions, her love, and her lust build. "I'm not sure I can resist," Jordan said huskily.

"Then don't."

Gazing deeply into Taylor's eyes, Jordan listened as their breathing grew labored. With the simple touch of a hand, she felt as if she might have an orgasm right there. The sheer intensity of Taylor's touch sent pulsations of heat through her entire body.

"Tell me what you feel," Taylor said with a wicked grin.

"I feel everything," Jordan said. "There aren't really words for it."

"Put words to it. Tell me what you feel, what you think, and what you want."

The challenge in Taylor's tone sent a fresh set of chills through her. With a single wink from Taylor, Jordan felt all resolve leave her body. There was nothing wrong in this situation, except for the fact that Taylor was too far away from her.

"I feel like I can't wait to have you slide across this couch. I think that I love you. And, all I want is to be yours."

With a sideways grin, Taylor moved closer to Jordan, taking her in her arms.

"Are you sure?"

"I've never been more sure of anything in my life. I want you."

Deciding not to give Taylor the option of holding out, Jordan wrapped her arms around Taylor's neck and pulled her in closer. Stopping just short of a kiss, Jordan used her tongue to trace the pattern of Taylor's lip and pulled the bottom lip into her mouth, gently sucking and listening as a small moan escaped from Taylor's lips.

Throwing caution to the wind, she dove in to deepen the kiss. As their lips danced against each other, she felt her passion grow to the point that she could no longer resist.

Weaving the fabric of the bottom of Taylor's shirt in her fingers, she pulled back to look into Taylor's eyes.

"May I?"

"Please do," Taylor said, lust glazing her eyes.

Not waiting for any further invitation, Jordan pulled the shirt off in one swift motion and reached back to unhook Taylor's bra. Staring at her beautiful breasts as they sprang free, Jordan knew there was no denying what she felt—what she knew about herself.

As she gently sucked Taylor's already hardened nipple, Taylor threw her head back and let out a sigh of pleasure, lost in her longing.

She practically tore away Jordan's clothes until they both lay naked. Body against body, they moved rhythmically, and Jordan felt uninhibited ecstasy flood her body.

When Taylor's mouth found its way to her most intimate places, Jordan gave in with a loud cry. Afterward, Taylor came back up beside her, laying skin on skin as their breathing returned to normal.

"I love you," Jordan whispered, pressing her lips to Taylor's forehead.

"I love you, too."

"That's all that matters, isn't it?" Jordan asked, knowing the answer before it was spoken.

"It's all that matters to me. You're all that matters to me."

Wrapping her arms tighter around Taylor, she knew that truth had been spoken. It didn't matter what her parents thought or what anyone in this small community thought. It didn't matter what she had been taught, or all the derogatory remarks she had heard about "the gays" over the years. None of it mattered, except for the fact that she had found the one who made her soul come alive and dance. She had found the person who understood the depths of her being—her one in seven billion.

Contented, she sighed peacefully, even though the questions of how to make it work still lingered in the back of her mind.

"We will get through whatever comes," Taylor said, tracing Jordan's jawline with her fingertips. "My parents already know. I came out to them, and they're not thrilled—but they'll learn to live with it. Your mom has an idea of what's going on in your life, and the rest of the world can deal with it. It's none of their damn business anyway."

Jordan looked at Taylor in amazement. "You came out to them?"

Taylor's smile grew. "I did, because there's no reason to hide who I am. I love who I am, and I've accepted all the things that I was taught to hate. And, even more than that, I love you. Plain and simple. You love me. I don't throw that word around, and I'm pretty sure you don't either. My love is deep and strong and not easily shaken. It will take a lot more than the judgment of small-town America to ruin something this rare and precious."

Jordan nodded, hoping that Taylor's stubbornness and strength would lend itself to her. These days, she felt anything but strong. But, she was in love. That much was certain, and she was willing to fight for it.

"I promise you we will be okay. We can make this work, and I know we can make each other so much happier together than we would be if we fought it."

"I know," Jordan said. "I've done a lot of thinking, and I know it's ridiculous to keep fighting it like this. You're everything I've ever wanted, and so many things I never even imagined I needed. I want to be with you, I want to be everything you need, too."

Taylor kissed her on the forehead, and Jordan felt her body relax for the first time in weeks. Every bit of tension released as she breathed in the sweet smell of Taylor's perfume. No longer able to keep her eyes open, she rested her head on Taylor's chest and fell into a deep sleep.

Jordan wasn't sure how much time had passed, but when she heard an angry pounding on the door, she woke with a start. Trying to adjust her eyes to the darkened room, she looked around and realized she was in Taylor's living room.

"Shit!" she exclaimed. "How long have I been asleep?"

Taylor emerged from the back room. "Keep your voice down," she said quietly. "We have a visitor, who I'm guessing is here looking for you."

The pounding continued. "Open the door," Janelle's voice boomed through the room.

Jordan's momentary disorientation faded as she remembered that she had places she was supposed to be, and now there was no doubt she would have questions to answer.

She looked down and realized that she was still stark naked. Quickly, she put on her clothes and attempted to make herself look more collected.

"My car is outside," Jordan said, realizing she had nowhere to run. "I'm sure she's already seen it."

Taking a deep breath, Jordan opened the door, glancing back only slightly to silently tell Taylor it was something they had to face.

"What are you doing here?" Janelle demanded.

"I'm figuring things out on my own, like any grown woman should have the chance to do," Jordan said boldly.

"You're not a grown woman," Janelle spat. "You're just a confused child being led astray by this monster."

She pointed a finger in Taylor's direction. "What do you think you're doing to this poor girl?"

"Nothing she doesn't want, I assure you," Taylor said. "Why are you at my house? You have no right to be here."

"This doesn't concern you," Janelle said, turning her attention back to Jordan. "This is just between me and Jordan."

"Actually, it does concern me," Taylor said, stepping beside Jordan and putting her arm around her. "This is my house, and this is my best friend. What can we help you with?"

"To start with, you can get your hands off her," Janelle snapped.

Taylor laughed, but Jordan was too caught up in the confrontation to find humor in the situation.

"She's an adult. She can make her own decisions. I don't speak for her, and neither do you."

Taylor turned to face Jordan. "Do you want to go back to Janelle's house?" she asked.

Jordan shook her head.

"I think you should go then," Taylor said to Janelle.

"I won't give up that easy—not when there's so much at stake."

"What is there at stake for you?" Jordan asked. "What does it matter to you?"

Before Janelle could answer, Jordan continued. "Don't you dare say that it's out of concern for my family, because I know it's not. You have some kind of superhero complex, or something. It's either that, or you feel the need to have a project, but I refuse to be your project. I won't allow you try to mold me into a little replica robot of you. I have my own thought process. I'm not nearly as fucked up as you think I am. In fact, you're the one with some psychological issues that you need to work through on your own—or maybe you need therapy. Either way, I can't do this anymore. This isn't working out for me, and all you do is tear me down and mess with my head. I'm going to do things my way, and I'm going to be happy."

Janelle stood angry and fuming, obviously searching for the right words to say.

"I'll be by tomorrow to get the rest of my things," Jordan said. "Have a good night."

With that, she shut the door and turned the lock into place.

"Damn," Taylor commented with respect shining in her smile. "You handled that like a pro."

Jordan smiled, feeling freer than she had in days. She took a deep breath.

"You know that we will have to deal with everyone else soon. It isn't going to be an easy task."

"No," Taylor said in agreement. "But if it means I get to have you, it's worth it. Anything is worth having you."

CHAPTER SEVENTEEN

Knowing that she should be a more mature person—but also knowing full well that she couldn't resist—Callie Wilkins picked up her cell phone.

After receiving the juiciest bit of gossip she had ever heard, there was no way she could keep it to herself. Anxiously, she tapped her fingers on the table as she tried to decide who to call first. Of course, this was going to be a prayer request for "the families involved who were dealing with a tough time," but she knew in her heart that it would also be the one thing that she could use to get Taylor Reeves out of town once and for all.

There would be no more of Taylor's meddling in her young adults group, and there would be no more competing with her for anyone's attention. Callie would go back to being the queen bee, as she had always been before Taylor blazed into town with her perfect hair and charm.

This was exactly the type of situation for which Callie had been waiting. Her smile grew as she considered the fact that this situation was actually far better than anything she could have dreamed up on her own.

Setting her plan of destruction up in her mind, she dialed one of her favorite gossiping buddies.

Once she had placed five calls, asking women to pray for the families of Jordan Weston and Taylor Reeves, she sat back with contentment. Her work here was done, and it was only a matter of time until Taylor's world came crashing down around her.

* * *

With the door closed and locked, the outside world ceased to matter. Jordan watched as Taylor popped the cork on a bottle of champagne.

"What are we celebrating?" Jordan asked with a knowing smile.

"We're celebrating the fact that I'm with you tonight, and the fact that I'm going to ask you to be my girlfriend."

Jordan felt her smile grow, and she knew instinctively that there would be no turning back after she agreed.

"Are you asking me now?" she asked, playfully.

"I am," Taylor said, handing her a glass.

"I'd love nothing more," Jordan said, raising her glass in the air. "Here's to my beautiful girlfriend, the girl who has turned my world upside down and taught me more about myself than I ever thought possible. Here's to her piercing blue eyes that somehow see into my soul and reveal truths I never knew. Here's to her lips that kiss me with such tenderness, and her touch that ignites unmatchable fire. Here's to the one I love."

Taylor's eyes widened with each statement and raised her glass in the air. "Here's to our love. Here's to us," she added before clinking her glass against Jordan's.

In one gulp, Jordan downed the glass and sat it on the table. She set her iPod up into Taylor's speakers and carefully selected a song.

"May I have this dance?" she asked with a wink, extending her hand to Taylor.

Taylor obliged, taking Jordan's hand in her own and standing to wrap her arms around Jordan's waist. Swaying with the beat, with their bodies pressed together, Jordan was confident that time was standing still. There had never been a moment in time more perfect. Of that she was absolutely certain.

"What happens next?" she asked, nuzzling her head against Taylor's neck.

"I suppose this is the part where we live happily ever after," Taylor joked.

"I don't think we're there yet," Jordan said with a laugh. "I don't think we've defeated the evil queen quite yet."

"Aw, yes," Taylor said in a silly voice. "The villain still remains. Don't worry about her, though. We'll take care of it all in due time."

Jordan didn't want to interrupt their evening, but she had no doubts that Janelle was plotting her revenge as they danced. The thought concerned her.

"As long as we face it together, it will be okay," Taylor said, stroking Jordan's hair and trying to soothe away her fears. "Stop worrying and dance with me."

Feeling her hesitation fade as she looked into Taylor's eyes, Jordan embraced the sweet surrender and decided to let tomorrow's worries come when they came. There was no sense in rushing it or worrying about it. What was going to happen would happen whether or not she spent all night obsessing over it, so while she had this precious opportunity to let Taylor's love completely wash over and intoxicate her, that's exactly what she was going to do.

As the early night hours faded into the early morning hours, Jordan lay awake in Taylor's arms. In between the long periods of silence, one of them would utter how happy she was and sleepily luxuriate in the simplicity of new love.

Jordan's phone beeped, pulling her from her cozy dreamlike state. Blinking, she glanced at the clock.

"What could be so important at three a.m.?"

Taylor shrugged and stifled a yawn.

"I'm not sure," she said, covering her mouth. "Better check it just in case it's something important. People don't usually text in the middle of the night for no reason."

Jordan reluctantly left the security of Taylor's bed and went to her dresser. She giggled as Taylor shot her bra across the room, hitting Jordan in the arm as she walked by the side of the bed.

But as she opened up the text message, all traces of humor disappeared. She felt the blood drain from her face.

"What is it?" Taylor asked, sitting up in bed and covering herself with the sheet.

"Apparently, I didn't hear the first several times it beeped," she said. "I have seven different messages here—from really random people. It looks like the gossip trail was burning hot tonight."

"What do they say?"

"They're all just pretty much asking me if it's true. They want to know if I'm a lesbian."

She steadied herself, taking a seat on the corner of the bed.

"Ignore them," Taylor advised.

"I plan on it," Jordan said, setting the phone down on the dresser.

"Then, what's wrong?"

She turned to face Taylor with amusement. "It's just that a few hours ago, I wouldn't have been able to answer that question—at least not without freaking out first. But, I know now, and I know that it's okay. It's not something dirty, and it's not wrong. It's who I am—who I've always been, and I'm proud of it. I'm not going to run and confirm everything that Janelle has been spreading, but I'm not going to run and hide either. I'm better than that. We are better than that. This love is something to be proud of—not something to run from and hide from the world."

Taylor smiled, and she felt more comfortable in her skin than she had ever felt before. Sure, there was bound to be fallout, but whatever came, she knew that she would have Taylor by her side.

Crawling back into bed, she pulled Taylor in for another kiss before they went to sleep.

"Thank you," Jordan whispered.

"Why are you thanking me?"

"You taught me what love means, and you taught me to love myself. That's the most important gift anyone has ever given me, and I don't know if I'll ever be able to adequately thank you. But you can bet I'm never going to stop trying."

Taylor rolled over playfully on top of Jordan.

"And I'll never stop trying to please you and make you happy," she said. "I think we'll both enjoy the challenge."

Alternating between giggling and kissing, they tumbled through the sheets. As Jordan soaked in the bliss of the moment, the truth resonated within her. She wasn't alone in the world, and it did not matter if no one else approved. She was who she was, and she had found the one who made her soul sing.

That was more than enough for her.

THREE MONTHS LATER

As Taylor loaded the last suitcase into her truck, the smile on her face grew.

"What are you thinking about, babe?" Jordan asked, sliding behind her and wrapping her hands around her waist to pull Taylor closer to her.

Taylor spun around in her arms and planted a quick kiss on Jordan's forehead. "How sweet it is to be with you, and how sweet justice can be."

Jordan raised an eyebrow in response, her green eyes twinkling with a hint of mischief. "Well, I was a little upset by how long it took, but you didn't think I was going to sit idly by and watch that woman tear everything apart for someone else? Justice was necessary."

Letting out a low, throaty, teasing growl, Taylor winked. "My baby sounds like a superhero. Serving up justice."

"Justice, for sure," Jordan said, wriggling her hips into Taylor's. "Justice, with a side of pleasure."

Laughing, they climbed into the truck together, headed for their getaway in Denver. When Taylor turned the key in the ignition, "Ironic" by Alanis Morissette played from the stereo, and they shared a satisfied smile.

"It's ironic that the two whose reputations she tried to smear are the same two who made sure she won't blackmail and torture another poor young girl, isn't it?" Jordan said with a playful shrug.

Taylor nodded. "Let's hit the road and put it all behind us for the week."

As they drove out of town, Taylor couldn't help but glance at the church as they circled the block. As if on cue, Janelle emerged from the back office, sour-faced and carrying a box of her belongings. Taylor's smile grew as she watched her father standing off to the side of the doorway, monitoring her every move.

When he'd found out all that she had done, there was no way he could keep her on staff. It had taken time, of course, for him to come around to the fact that what she'd done was wrong. But, with Jordan's persistence, and given the disapproval expressed by Jordan's family, he had finally seen the jeopardy in having someone on his staff who would practically kidnap and blackmail someone, forcing them into types of therapies she wasn't even licensed to perform.

While he had still argued that they both needed therapy, he'd eventually come to terms with the fact that Janelle had gone about it improperly.

"Do you think he'll ever come around?" Jordan asked, following Taylor's gaze.

Taylor shrugged. "Maybe. Maybe not. But, if nothing else, I know that deep down he still loves me. He took a stand against Janelle's actions. In and of itself it's a huge showing to the fact that to some degree his loyalties still lie with me."

Jordan reached for her hand and gave it a reassuring squeeze. Bringing it to her lips, she gave it a gentle kiss. "I think maybe he'll soften more as time goes on."

"Your parents have adjusted quite well—albeit not perfectly." Taylor felt a slight pang of jealousy at the way Jordan's parents still invited her to family dinners and surrounded her with love. It was love absent of support for their relationship, but it was love nonetheless. Even so, she was happy Jordan had that type of a support system, as shocking as it might have been for her family initially. "But, no matter what happens, I have you," Taylor added, completely satisfied by the thought.

"And I have you," Jordan said as they drove off, beaming in the glow that can only come from genuine bliss.

Bella Books, Inc.

Women. Books. Even Better Together.

P.O. Box 10543
Tallahassee, FL 32302

Phone: 800-729-4992
www.bellabooks.com